SILENT PRIMA DONNA

The Replacement Series

BOOK ONE

Gianna Marie Ferraro

Content warnings

This is a toxic historical romance.

Organized crime

Accidental pregnancy

Insinuated sexual assault

Mention of prostitution

Abuse

kidnapping

Murder

Violence

Shooting of police

Dysfunctional family

Cheating

Light smut

Age gap relationship

Illegal activities

Mention of drugs

Racism

Abuse of a minor

Minor burning of skin

Strong language

Generative AI disclosure

The author <u>did NOT use AI tools</u> in the ideation of writing, illustrating or editing of this work. If AI was used by third parties, such as editors, software developers or stock elements the usage was not disclosed to the author.

PART ONE

Prima and Nico

1960

CHAPTER ONE

PRIMA

Mamma said I was meant for great things. She had said the same thing about my sisters. We'd never had the chance to make our own choices. Marriage was no different.

My sister Silvia had been married off to a wealthy man in Vermont. I hadn't seen her since. She apparently had a two-year-old girl. She would send us money every month so Mamma wouldn't have to work.

My oldest sister, Stella, ran away when she turned sixteen. I received postcards from her now and again. I always figured she had moved in with my father since my parents had divorced around the same time.

I was like a silk glove to Mamma. That's what she would tell me, at least. I was always by her side.

Today would be the first time I would be away from Mamma in years. I had no clue if I would see her again.

August of 1953 was the last time I'd seen my father. Now, it was 1960, and I hadn't received so much as a letter from him in the last seven years. He would write to Mamma, mainly to send her money. It was either that or have the cops called on him. I didn't think anything he did was legal.

The last time he wrote was when he told my mamma that he had found me a husband. He wanted the best for us. Father probably didn't want to pay Mamma anymore either. Now it was time to face fate.

I was to marry a man I had never met. In exchange, Mamma would be given money. That was how it had been with Silvia too.

Mamma wanted me to be like any other modern woman, a housewife. I'd been raised to be a housewife. To cook, clean, and take care of future children, nothing more. I didn't mind the thought of being a housewife. What else would I be?

My heels clicked as I climbed the steps of the townhome, the address matching the paper my mamma had given me. My white lace gloves felt odd on the paper. I slid the paper into my black satin purse before clasping it shut. I took a deep breath before lightly knocking on the door.

I barely recognized my father when he opened the door. His brown hair was slicked back, grays peeking out. His eyes were blue and piercing. He smiled at me with a crooked smile. "There's my Prima!" He pulled me into a hug. "How old are you now? You've grown so much."

I hesitantly returned the hug. "Twenty-one."

He chuckled. "That long, huh? I probably look like an old man now." He smiled at me. "You look just like your mother. Hopefully less of a floozy." He cleared his throat "You're even more beautiful than the pictures she sent."

Everyone always said I looked Polish like my mother. My sisters looked more Italian. Both of my sisters had brown hair and blue eyes like my father. I had blonde hair and brown eyes like my mother, but I had a curvier figure. Most people said my mother looked like an older Marilyn Monroe.

My mother liked to keep me all dolled up. Today was no different even though she was thousands of miles away. With lace gloves, a light pink dress, and heels. Just how she liked me.

My father poured himself a drink of Johnny Walker as I sat down on the couch. It felt odd seeing him again. It was almost like he was a different person. He used to be so cold and distant.

"You know why you're here, right?" He sipped his drink and limped slightly as he walked to the couch, taking a seat.

I nodded. "To get married."

"Nico DeLuca saw one of those photos your mamma sent. She said to look out for a husband for you, and he seems to be the right man. He's definitely older than you, but I think it will be fine."

If that's what they wanted, that's what I would do. I had no purpose in life. At least that's what Mamma would say. Following orders was the one thing I seemed good at.

The fact he was older made my stomach churn. What was I to say? I had to marry him and that was that.

"He's rich, so of course your bitch of a mother would agree to it." He set his drink down.

I didn't remember much about the divorce. I did remember him always calling her a bitch. Stella used to get mad at them for yelling so much. I didn't like hearing it either.

"Why did you agree to the marriage?" I diverted my attention to my feet.

"He's a friend." My father shrugged. "And he has the money to take care of you. He owes me."

"What does he do?" I hesitantly asked.

"We are in the same business. We run the bus company around here. I'm his right-hand man." My father was being vague. Something about his tone made me think he was lying. Knowing him, he probably was.

"When do I meet him?" My eyes grazed my lap. I was in no rush to meet the man.

"Tonight. But you can't dress like that. Your mom always dressed you too . . . matronly."

My dress was longer than most women my age wore, with a boat neckline. I guessed you could call it matronly.

"Nico has an outfit picked out for you. He wants you to dress a certain way." My father poured himself another drink. He seemed more nervous to see me than anything. It seemed like he didn't know how to react around me anymore.

He took me to my room for the night, his drink in his hand. It was a modest room with a bed and a dresser. The walls were light blue. There was a blue dress lying on the white sheets.

"I'll leave you to get changed," he told me before closing the door.

The dress was tight on top. It was a knee-length navy-blue dress. The skirt flared out below the white belt. The neckline was a V-neck which showed off my chest more than I liked.

It was definitely not something Mamma would let me wear. I was uncomfortable with it too. I didn't like showing off my chest this much. Most women wore modest necklines. This was too much.

Gianna Marie Ferraro

NICO

Tonight, I would meet my wife. Not something I thought I'd be saying as a forty-three-year-old bachelor. I never thought I'd get married. Frankly, I never wanted to.

I was respected around here. As the head of the family, this neighborhood belonged to me.

All the ladies around my age loved to fuck me—or at least acted like it. They always told me I was a real flutter bum. Getting married hadn't necessarily been my plan for life. But I owed Vinnie.

"Boss, you good?" Enzo questioned as he handed me a cup of espresso.

Enzo was one of my soldiers. He was also my errand boy. He did whatever I told him, whenever I told him, even if his hands got dirty. He was young and determined to make it in my world.

It helped that his Uncle Zeno was in charge before me. He had told me to take care of Enzo, so that's what I did. He was a good kid.

"Yeah, I'm fine." I was staring off. The bar was oddly quiet today.

"Are you excited for tonight?" Enzo sat next to me with his own shot of espresso.

"I guess so."

I didn't know how to feel. Part of me felt like my freedom was being taken away, but the other half was happy to settle down.

I was more nervous about how she would fit in being mobbed up.

"You need to dress better than that," I told Enzo, looking at his messed-up buttons and missing sports coat. "You won't get any respect."

"Sorry, sir, I was in a rush this morning," Enzo replied as he fixed his buttons.

"You finally fuck Pat last night?" I joked.

He blushed. "No, I didn't. I slept in, that's all." He rubbed the back of his neck. "So . . . what's the girl's name? Vinnie's daughter."

"Prima." I pulled a photo out of my suit pocket. I didn't know why I kept it there.

"She's a fine looking broad. Looks young." Enzo lit a cigarette.

"Only twenty-one." I chuckled. "She's willing to marry me. That's all I care about."

Enzo had a surprised look on his face. "And Vinnie is okay with that?"

"Yeah, I guess. I'm marrying her, aren't I?" I lit a cigarette of my own and blew the smoke in his face, causing him to cough.

I owed him, after all. It was the least I could do. Why he would give me his youngest daughter was beyond me. Did I want to get married? Not really. But at least she was a looker.

19

Gianna Marie Ferraro

prima

We made it to the entrance of the club, Burtos'. It was apparently very popular. Men and women lined up outside the brick building, but next to my father, I got right in.

We entered into what seemed to be the entryway with a coat check.

My father waved to a man. "Nico!"

The man I assumed was Nico stood by the coat check. He perked up at hearing my father's voice.

"Vinnie!" The man came over and gave my father a hug and a polite kiss on the cheek. He looked me up and down before grabbing my hand. "This must be the lovely Prima." He bit his lip.

Nico was definitely much older than me, not much younger than my father. He had dark brown hair and eyes that pierced into your soul. They almost looked black. He was tall and intimidating to look at. He was handsome for an older man, I had to admit.

It felt strange knowing that this was the man I was supposed to marry. I knew nothing about him. I felt slightly uneasy.

He didn't let go of my hand, dragging me along as he walked. "Let's go to the main room, shall we?"

The club had white walls that brightened the room despite the dim lighting. There were green curtains draped along them. A band was playing on a stage toward the front of the room.

The song *"Old Black Magic"* boomed in the other room as people danced on the dance floor. Nico pulled me on the floor, placing his hands on my waist and mine on his shoulders as he swayed me back and forth. His touch barely phased me.

"You're prettier in person. I didn't think that was possible" He chuckled as he spun me around. I thought he was trying to talk to me at one point, but I could barely hear him.

Nico pulled me close to him. "You don't talk much, do you?"

"It's too loud to talk." I waved a hand toward the band.

"Maybe we can take a step outside."

We told my father before heading out. As we stood on the sidewalk, I noticed that the line into the club had gotten shorter.

I felt cold in the summer heat. My heart was racing as we stood next to each other.

Nico pulled out a pack of cigarettes and lit one. "So, Prima, what do you do for fun?"

What did I do for fun? I took care of Mamma. That was pretty much it. "Read . . . " was all I could think of.

"Read?" He scoffed. "Well, I guess I can get you some books." He messed with his shirt collar and changed the subject "Are you ready to get married tomorrow?"

"Tomorrow?" My stomach dropped.

"Yeah, I know it's soon."

Tomorrow? Father hadn't said anything about getting married so soon. I just got here. I barely knew Nico and now I was expected to get married right away.

"C-can I ask you something?" I stuttered out.

"Sure, why not."

"Why me?"

He smiled and took a lock of my hair in his fingers. "Now's not the time for that. Let's go back inside."

Gianna Marie Ferraro

NICO

My god, she was gorgeous, a real piece of ass. And she was all mine. Her curves were in all the right places. Her skin was so soft to the touch. Her hair was a beautiful shade of gold, and her brown eyes were doe-like.

The only thing that was shitty was that she looked so much like her mother. Except her mother looked like she hadn't eaten in a week and barely had any curves.

Her mother had always tried to come onto me, but I'd never let her touch me. Vinnie was too good of a friend to ruin his marriage. They had done that on their own.

Not that Vinnie had stayed loyal, but Cathleen would sleep with any man that looked her way. She never cared about Vinnie's feelings.

Prima was so timid and shy. She barely talked the whole night. After we got back inside, she sat next to me at a table and watched the band, my arm around her shoulders. I could feel her tapping her foot to the music under the table.

No one batted an eye at seeing me with a younger woman. They all knew me. They probably thought she was tonight's fling.

"You excited to fuck my daughter?" Vinnie laughed.

Prima's face turned bright red.

"Vinnie, how drunk are you?" I laughed. I was embarrassed for the girl. But I was used to Vinnie being drunk. He never got this drunk though. He must've been nervous seeing us together.

"Very." Vinnie took a swig of his drink. He had been drinking since we got there.

"Pull yourself together" I mumbled to him.

I noticed Vinnie's smile drop as he looked across the room. Ray Gallo sat at a table with his boneheaded son, Frank. Ray ran another part of town. We tried to stay away from each other to keep the peace. Sure, I had sent him flowers when his wife died, and our families got along, but I'd never want to have dinner with that man. It was strictly business. I hadn't gotten along with Ray since childhood.

"Prima, you look tired. Vinnie, you two should go home," I told them before standing up.

Prima got up from her seat and followed Vinnie outside without any protest. She seemed obedient.

I noticed Ray and he noticed me. I sent him a glare before following the two outside. I was not going to ruin my night.

Gianna Marie Ferraro

pRiMA

I stared at the ceiling as I sunk into the bed at my father's townhouse. He had two bedrooms. Why? I didn't know.

All I knew was that I had to get married in the morning. Why would he want to marry me? Didn't men like him stay single their whole lives?

Nico reminded me of a gangster. I wouldn't doubt if he was one given how my father had talked about him. My mother said he was a rich man with a business. It seemed that was the only answer I was going to get.

I didn't know how I felt about marrying Nico. It was another choice Mamma had made on my behalf, nothing more.

I went to public school in New York until I turned eight. I didn't remember much. Mamma homeschooled all of us after that, which mainly consisted of us reading. She said school kids would cause us to go mad if we stayed in school. Father never agreed with it. That was probably part of the reason he'd left us.

There wasn't a day they weren't screaming at each other. My sisters and I would sit in our room reading or playing games, trying not to listen to them fight. I remembered them arguing about who Stella would marry. Then she left a note a week later saying she ran away. Father left a week after that. That's why I assumed she eventually went with him.

I was stuck at home back then, and now, I was stuck here. I could've run away if I really wanted. *Would they come after me?*

I would never have the strength to leave. I was taught to stay put and silent. So, I did what I did best.

CHAPTER TWO

PRIMA

I wore a tea length wedding dress with lace across the bodice and a tulle skirt. It was honestly quite beautiful and fit like a glove. Adorned with white lace gloves to match.

We were in a quaint church in the middle of the neighborhood. The church wasn't decorated for the wedding. It was almost like they wanted to get it over with.

I blacked out for most of the ceremony, saying "I do" when asked to. The kiss felt off. I put on a fake smile as I faced my father, some of his friends, and their wives.

When we left the church, people stared, but no one said a word, at least not to our faces. I could hear people murmur as we walked to the car. It must've looked odd seeing an older man with a young woman in a wedding dress.

Nico let go of my hand before walking over to my father, saying something in his ear. Then they embraced for a moment before Nico came back to me. "Come on, let's take you home." Nico smiled.

He grabbed my hand oddly, gently, like I was made of glass, once more before taking me to his car.

I was a married woman now. I didn't know if I was happy. I felt nothing. Everything was fuzzy.

Gianna Marie Ferraro

NICO

I was sweating. I could've backed out at any time. She couldn't. I was wearing a black suit and tie. I just threw it on. What else was I going to wear? No one would give a fuck. I was the groom. It was so strange to think of it that way.

When she walked down the aisle, I could see her shaking. She looked beautiful. So pure and innocent like an angel.

Vinnie was sitting near me. He didn't feel comfortable walking her down. He barely knew Prima anymore. But he had a huge grin on his face. I was surprised he was okay with this marriage. He used to complain to me about how Cathleen used to set up his older daughters. Now I was marrying his baby.

I looked at the small woman in front of me and took her hands as the priest instructed us to say our vows; it was too late now.

I wasn't scared to marry her. I was scared about the freedom I was going to lose.

Gianna Marie Ferraro

PRIMA

We drove for a few minutes in Nico's new shiny white nineteen fifty-nine Cadillac. I only knew what kind of car it was because he told me.

I watched out the window, taking in the sights of my new neighborhood. Kids played on the street as their mothers yelled at them to come in for lunch. Men drank on the sidewalk and talked amongst themselves. It reminded me of my childhood.

The neighborhood seemed to get nicer the farther we went. There were more businessmen and women with baby carriages walking around. It was completely different. A small park was next to a row of townhouses. We stopped on the side of the road in front of one. The townhouse he lived in was larger than my father's, by at least two rooms.

We hopped out of the car and walked up to the stone steps. Nico scooped me up once we reached the stairs by the entrance, carrying me inside like a real bride. He put me down in the living room. I felt nothing.

"What do you think?" he questioned.

I took it all in for a moment. "It's nice."

The living room looked as if he'd bought it with all the furniture already inside. The furniture was more mid-century modern than what my father had. The walls were painted light green. A blue couch and armchair were set in front of a large television. It had to be at least twenty-one inches. There were pictures of what I assumed was his family on the walls, with no other artwork.

"You can redecorate anytime you want," he told me. "I have a maid come in three times a week so don't worry too much about cleaning."

He grabbed my hands, taking my white gloves off. "We want to keep these beautiful hands of yours in good shape. You'll go to the salon once a week, okay?"

"Okay . . . " I looked away from his piercing gaze, and he scooped me up again, carrying me to the bedroom. He set me down once more.

"Let's take that dress off, see what I got myself into." He chuckled.

He disappeared behind me, kissing my neck as he unbuttoned the back of my dress. My dress slid to the floor, followed by my slip. Then he stopped for a moment, spinning me around to look at him.

"What's that scar on your back from?" he queried.

I had a large scar down my back, along my spine, that started under my shoulder blades. I ignored his question, pulling him into a kiss like I'd been taught to do. That seemed to do the trick. He grabbed my waist and placed me on the bed. The rest of my clothes ended up on the floor

A chill ran down my spine as he took off his belt and undid his pants. He pressed his lips against mine, laying me down on the bed.

Nico raised a brow. "Prima, have you done this before?"

I pulled him into another kiss, not wanting to answer.

When he was finished, he sat next to me, before pulling me on his lap. "You don't have to fake anything with me, Prima. I know being my wife isn't what you wanted."

"What else am I supposed to do?" I replied quietly.

I did what I was told. That's how I was raised, to be obedient. Why did he have an issue with that? Isn't that what all men wanted? A wife that did what she was told?

He grabbed my chin, making me look at him. "What happened before you came here?"

I felt tears start to slip down my cheeks. I didn't remember the last time I'd cried. I could feel myself starting to shake. He whipped a tear away with his thumb before laying me back on the bed.

"You can tell me in the morning." He got up and grabbed some clothes, leaving the room.

Gianna Marie Ferraro

NICO

I sat alone in the living room with a glass of Royal Brackla in my hand. It was probably one of my favorite drinks. I loved how it burned as it went down my throat. It made me feel something.

I didn't finish putting my clothes back on. I sat there in my boxers and drank. What was that scar on Prima's back from? Would she even tell me?

It looked too deep to be an accident, and trust me, I would know. I let out a sigh and made my way back to the bedroom, leaving the dirty whisky glass on the coffee table.

I couldn't help but smile seeing the beautiful woman in my bed. She had the skin of an angel and the most beautiful soft hair. She was stunning even when she slept.

I lay down next to her, keeping my distance. I didn't want to scare her too much on the first night. She was my wife now, but I didn't know her.

When I woke up, I could smell bacon. I groaned as I got out of bed, unable to tell if I was hungover or just old.

I slipped some clothes on before making my way to the kitchen. Prima was sitting at the table with two plates of food, one across from her. She ate alone

quietly as I placed my hands on her shoulders.

45

Gianna Marie Ferraro

prima

I placed a plate of eggs and bacon on the table. I sat down across from it with a plate for myself and ate quietly. I jumped when I felt hands on my shoulders. I wasn't expecting Nico to be up so early, especially since he had been up most of the night.

"You made breakfast?" Nico smiled as he sat down.

"Yeah . . ."

The fridge was full of food. I didn't know what else to do with my time.

I gazed at my plate. "Made you a plate . . ."

"Thank you," he told me as he started to eat.

We ate in silence for a while. I barely touched the food on my plate. Nico's was empty before he started talking. "Are you ready to talk this morning?"

"I-I don't know." I got up and started to clean off the plates.

No, I didn't want to talk. Why did my past matter so much to him? Would he kick me out? My past was irrelevant. He didn't need to know what had happened.

Nico tapped his fingers on the table. "If I asked your father, would he tell me?"

"He doesn't know anything." I felt tears swell up.

"Prima, I know you don't know me, but I need you to be honest with me. I am your husband, after all." I could hear him tap his foot. "You weren't a virgin like your pops said, were you?"

"It's not like you think," I managed to say, putting the dirty dishes in the sink.

Nico's voice switched from calm to vexed. "What is it then? You didn't have someone before me, did you? You have a secret kid or something? Tell me before I make you."

How would he make me? I didn't want to find out. "Mamma would say my sister never sent enough money." I couldn't look at him. I continued staring into the sink, my heart beating out of my chest. "She had men over who would pay to—" I couldn't finish my sentence. My throat felt like it was closing. "Please don't kick me out."

I felt a gentle touch. He spun me around to look at him. His gaze was sorrowful.

"I'm the only one who will touch you from now on, okay? Anyone else does, you tell me, got it? I ain't going to do that to you. I don't give a fuck who touched you before. Now you're mine." He looked at his watch. "I need to have a chat with Vinnie. Go get dressed. I have a closet full of clothes for you in our bedroom."

I messed with the strings on my dressing gown, before hurrying to the bedroom. Why didn't he care? Didn't all men want virgins? I felt disgusting. Mamma had told me I was going to marry an older man because no one else would want me. Was she right?

He said I was his. I guessed he was right. I was his wife, after all.

I opened the closet door and found it packed full of dresses, blouses, and skirts, amongst other things. I grabbed a light pink dress, slipping it on quickly. It fit like a glove. Mamma must've given him my measurements. That explained why she'd measured me a few months ago.

Gianna Marie Ferraro

NICO

My blood was boiling as I entered the bar with Prima. *Why would that bitch do that to her own daughter?* Prostitute her out like that. I knew that Cathleen was a money-grabbing whore, but I didn't think she would stoop that low.

Unlike Vinnie, Cathleen would do anything to get money. That's probably why she'd married him in the first place. Vinnie had been rising up in the ranks of the underworld, and she'd wanted a piece of the cash.

I left Prima alone at a table to talk to Vinnie. If he had known about this, I would kill him. Prima was mine now.

"What is it, Nico? Why do you look so sour? Have a bad time last night?" Vinnie brought his attention to me, along with some other men at the table.

I ushered the other men away. "Vinnie, we need to talk."

"What? What happened?"

I sat down next to him and kept my voice low. "You know that wife of yours?"

"Ex-wife, yeah. What about her?" He smoothed down his gelled hair.

"Prima told me something I can't let go."

"Cut to the chase, Nico." Vinnie rolled his eyes.

"Apparently, Cathleen was whoring out your daughter for extra cash," I told him bitterly.

I watched as the man's face went from slightly amused to bright red.

"Why didn't you tell me, Vincenzo?!" I shouted.

"I didn't know what her whore mother was doing! You think I'd marry her to you if I did?" he spat back.

"That's not the problem. That broad of yours comes down here, I'll kill her." I glared.

"Do whatever the fuck you want. I hate that floozy," Vinnie replied. "I have things to take care of."

I was angry. Not at Vinnie but at Cathleen. Vinnie hadn't been there; he didn't know. But if he had been there, maybe he could've stopped her.

"I'm a terrible father, I know."I was never there for my girls. I probably never will be at this point." He leaned back in his chair. "But if I knew . . . "

"She messed with my property," I hissed. "The bitch will pay if she comes near her again, I swear."

55

Gianna Marie Ferraro

PRIMA

The bar was oddly quiet for it being almost full. People were talking, but I couldn't hear a thing. My silence was interrupted by Nico.

The men bickered for a few minutes at another table. They talked as if I weren't there. Most people did that. I could hear the crowd murmuring.

"I'm surprised he even got married, and to someone so young," one woman huffed.

"She's right there. She can hear you," the other woman mumbled loudly.

"Look at her, she won't do shit."

They were right; I wouldn't do anything. They went quiet as Nico stormed away and came to sit next to me. He lit a cigarette, blowing the smoke away from me. "Lorenzo! Grab me a drink."

A skinny brown-haired man around my age came over with a tray of drinks, placing one in front of Nico. The server dressed plain but his clothes were clean.

"Prima, this is Enzo. He works for me. Enzo, this is my new wife."

"Nice to meet you." Enzo smiled. "Does she want anything?"

"You want anything to drink?" Nico reiterated.

"I'm okay," I replied.

Enzo smiled warmly and changed the subject. "I'm surprised you two didn't go on a honeymoon, Mr. DeLuca."

Nico took a swig of his drink. "Too much work to do. I can't walk away right now. Maybe in a month."

"About that, did you still want me to—" Enzo started but Nico cut him off with a glare before speaking.

"Don't talk about work in front of my wife, got it? Don't be a jerk-off. Get out of here," he snapped.

"Of course, Mr. DeLuca." Enzo complied and walked off.

I fiddled with the hem of my dress and kept my gaze on the table. There was a cut right in the middle. I kept wondering what happened to cause the cut. I keep imagining someone's hand getting stabbed to the table.

Nico snapped me out of my demented daydream. "Anywhere you want to go for a honeymoon?" I watched him finish his drink.

"Anywhere is fine."

"You're a real flat tire, aren't you?" he chuckled. "Guess I didn't marry you for your personality."

I had no personality or opinions. That is what Mamma would always say. I was a silent Prima Donna, as she would call me. Beautiful, but wouldn't make a sound.

"I'll plan something," Nico hummed. "Maybe"—he placed a hand on my thigh— "tomorrow, you can go to the salon, maybe make a friend or two and get your hair done. Let's go to dinner tonight, just you and me."

The curtains of the private room of the restaurant were red like the rest of the room. A few plants were set around the room which didn't match the tasteful crystal lighting.

I twirled my pasta around. I barely ate anything. My stomach was rumbling but I didn't want to eat. Mamma would say it was better to not eat anyway.

"I wanted to lay down some rules." Nico shoved a piece of steak in his mouth. "I want you to be honest with me at all times, got it?"

"What about you?" I questioned.

"I'll be as honest as I can be." He took a sip of wine. "You're my wife, so people are going to look at you differently. If anyone disrespects you, you tell me immediately."

"Got it." I spooned the pasta into my mouth. I had to eat something.

"I know you probably didn't want to marry an old man like me." He placed a hand on my thigh. "Please try to like it here."

A waitress entered through the curtain separating the room from the rest of the restaurant. Nico pulled his hand away as she smiled and poured more wine into our glasses. "Anything else for you, Mr. DeLuca?" she questioned.

"I think a check soon," he told her.

"Anything else for you, Miss?"

"It's Mrs. DeLuca," Nico snapped.

"Oh, sorry, sir." The woman looked shocked.

"Get that look off your face. No respect." Nico shook his head.

"Is something wrong, Mr. DeLuca?" A man came practically out of nowhere.

"Yeah, this broad was disrespecting my wife." Nico huffed.

I would've spoken up, but I couldn't. I didn't know how to. I watched as the two men berated the poor girl in front of me. What could I say?

When we got home, I told Nico I wanted to take a bath. I watched the water run as I thought about that poor waitress at dinner.

The bath was lukewarm when I got in. I had looked in the mirror too long, trying to see what Nico saw in me, why he picked me. I had always been called beautiful, but I didn't see it. I wasn't a size one like my mamma. I swear one of my eyes was slightly lower than the other.

I dunked my head under the water, letting my curls fall flat. I didn't want to come up. I held my breath until I couldn't hold it anymore. I needed to feel something. Nico was standing there, watching me. He kneeled down next to the tub, swishing his hand in the water.

"How did you get your scar?" he quired.

"You ask a lot of questions about me, and I know nothing about you." I covered my chest with a washcloth.

He smiled. "Well, let's play a game then. I ask a question, then you do."

"Can I finish my bath first?"

Nico bit his lip. "Fine."

Gianna Marie Ferraro

63

NICO

The way Prima was comfortable being naked around me was odd. I guessed, considering her past, I shouldn't have been shocked. It's not like she was trying to be sexy either. She took her clothes off like it was nothing. Or, like earlier, she would sit in the tub and act like it was normal to have me sitting there.

Prima's hair was straight when she walked out of the bathroom.

"That your natural hair?" I questioned. I sat relaxed on the couch, in a white T-shirt and boxers.

"That's your first question?" She asked, taking a seat next to me. "Yes, it is . . . I figured I'd leave it straight since I'm going to the salon tomorrow anyway."

"Makes sense, women and their looks."

"What do you actually do for work?" she hesitantly asked.

"I run the buses around here. I make money. That's all you need to know."

Prima kept quiet.

She didn't need to know about the family business. My guess was that she already knew and didn't want to say it out loud. It wasn't like most women wanted to admit they were married to a mobster like me.

I wasn't interested in a woman who wanted to know about business.

I turned toward her and leaned in slightly. "What's with the scar on your back?"

She froze for a moment. "One of the men got mad at me, said I wasn't up to standard. So, he took a knife—"

She cut herself off and glanced at her lap.

I didn't know how to feel at that moment. I wanted to punch someone, but I also wanted to hug her. Instead, I grabbed a strand of her hair to play with and said, "Your turn" softly.

"Why me?" she quickly asked, finally looking at me.

"Do you ever smile? I've never seen you smile."

"Can you please answer?"

I frowned. "You really want the truth?"

She hesitantly replied, "yes."

"A man tried to kill me a year ago, and your father, who you may have noticed has a limp, jumped in front of the crossfire. Got hit right in the hip. Fucked up his leg for a while." He rubbed the back of his neck. "I owed him. One day, he showed me your photo and said your mother was looking for a husband for you. I'd been a bachelor for a long time and thought I'd settle down and repay a debt."

"So, I'm here to help you pay your debt?"

"I thought you were too beautiful to pass up."

I pinned her to the couch, fear on her face. It felt good. I ran my hands down her arms, her skin so soft, before getting up.

"You don't have to love me, but you're stuck with me, babe." I walked toward the bedroom. "I'm going to go out. Get some rest."

After our little game, I met up with some guys for a few drinks at a club. I sat alone at a table as I watched them dance with fine dames. I would normally be up there dancing.

A woman who looked around my age made her way to the table, placing her hand on it next to me. Her large jugs were inches from my face.

She was a cheap looking broad in a cheetah print blouse and tight black skirt. Her hair was brown and curled. You could smell the cheap perfume from a mile away.

"Hey stud." She winked. "Want to dance?"

"Not in the mood, lady," I told her.

"Come on, dance with me!" She flashed me a crooked smile and grabbed my hand. She wasn't very pretty, but she did have nice tits. A dance couldn't hurt, right?

I made my way to the dance floor with the big breasted woman. We danced for a while before I spun her around. Then she pulled me close and kissed me.

I was not proud of cheating on my wife on our second day of being married. But as a man with power here, the ladies could never keep their hands off me. How could I have said no?

I stumbled into the kitchen to grab a glass of water. I was definitely going to be hungover tomorrow. I didn't even notice that the light in the kitchen was already on when I entered.

I spun around with a glass of water in hand. Prima was sitting at the table with a book. "Hi, Nico . . . Have a good time?" She kept her eyes low.

"Yeah," I hiccupped. "It's late, what are you doing?"

"Couldn't sleep . . . "

She was in this lovely light blue nightgown that I'd gotten for her. It had lace on the top that formed a V-neck. It clung to her body, showing every curve. I grabbed her waist and turned her around, bending her over the table.

CHAPTER THREE

PRIMA

I tried to ignore the fact that Nico smelled like another woman's perfume last night as I entered the salon.

The salon was packed with women of all ages. A hideous shade of bubblegum pink covered the walls and furniture. The joy seemed to be sucked out of it as soon as I entered, everyone quieting down as I walked up to the front counter.

"Hi, uh, I think I have an appointment under DeLuca?" I kept my focus down and tried to ignore the murmurs.

The woman at the counter popped the bubble gum she was chewing. She had brown hair that was styled nicely in a bob and an annoyed look on her face. She opened a booklet. "Yup, full treatment, huh? Guess that's what happens when you marry a gangster."

"Oh, hush, Barbra." A redheaded woman rolled her eyes. "Don't get your panties in a twist. Your mouth will get you into trouble."

"The smartass redhead over there is Pat. She'll be taking care of you." Barbra pointed at her before going back to reading a magazine.

Pat greeted me with a warm smile. I walked over to her chair and sat down. Pat draped a cape over my shoulders. "What do you want done, hun?"

"Just styled, I think," I replied shyly.

She handed me a magazine. "Here, look through this."

I flipped through it for a moment before pointing to a picture of a woman with wavy hair. The model had long blonde hair just like me. "This one would be nice . . ."

Pat smiled. "Should be easy enough."

I stayed quiet as she styled my hair. The room grew louder the less I talked. I wasn't used to the amount of attention that being Nico's wife gave me. I hated it.

"So, you're Nico's new wife." Pat smiled as she put a roller in my hair.

"Yeah . . ."

"How old are you? If you don't mind my asking"

I kept my gaze on the mirror in front of me.

"Twenty-one," I replied finally.

"Shit, I'm older than you, kid." She chuckled.

Barbra butted in, "What do you like about him? He fuck good?"

"Barb, stop being jealous. We all know you have a thing for Nico," Pat snapped.

"What woman over the age of thirty doesn't? He's a sexy man." Barbra popped her gum.

"Guess he's popular." I shuffled slightly in the chair.

The thought of Nico being with another woman last night crossed my mind. I tried to push the thought out of my head.

Pat placed another roller in my hair. "You aren't from around here, hun, are ya?"

"I haven't lived here since I was little . . ."

She leaned in. "Nico is feared around here, that's all I can say," she murmured in my ear.

Gianna Marie Ferraro

NICO

I was definitely hungover. I drank a bitter black coffee as Vinnie jabbed about his conquests of the night. Enzo sat next to him quietly with a cup of his own.

I still felt groggy even though this was my third cup of coffee. I didn't remember even drinking that much last night.

We were sitting at Donny's restaurant. It was already lunchtime, but the restaurant was empty, aside from us. Donny had closed it down for us. I didn't want all that noise. I didn't order anything to eat; I was too nauseous. At least the coffee was something.

I looked at Vinnie when he mumbled to me. "The fuck is he doing here?"

I brought my attention to a skinny, pale man. His light brown hair was slicked back with gel. It was Ray Gallo's son, Frank. He sat at a table with one of his guys. They never came around here unless they wanted something from me.

"The restaurant's closed," Enzo spoke up.

They ignored us as Frank kept staring at me from across the room. His associate was whispering something to him before Frank stood up and made his way over to our table. His associate watched him walk over before leaving for the bathroom.

"Nico, good to see you." He smiled sheepishly.

"What do you want, Frank?" I wasn't in the mood for his shit.

"My father wanted me to talk to you about—"

I cut him off. "If your father wants something then he has to tell me himself. Don't make me paint the sidewalk with your face."

"Nico, come on."

"That's Don DeLuca to you," Enzo snapped at him.

"We want to buy this fine establishment out," Frank told me.

"No way in hell. Zeno owned Donny's." My voice almost growled. There was no way in hell I would give this place up, especially not to Ray. Zeno was like a god to us. Before me, there was Zeno. I was God around here now. There was no way in hell I would give a piece of my heaven to Ray.

"Why do you want it anyway, kid?" Vinnie questioned him.

"That's none of your damn business," Frank snapped.

I stood up. I was slightly taller than him, so I could almost stare him in the eyes. I didn't see him grab

Vinnie's beer bottle until he slammed it on the table, breaking it. I almost dodged it, but he ended up slamming it into my shoulder.

If I had been wearing my suit jacket, I would've been fine. But now I had a piece of glass lodged in my shoulder, sticking out slightly.

I grabbed Frank's head, slamming it down on the table, before pulling out my gun. I shot him in the back of the leg and then the shoulder.

"Why'd you shoot him twice?!" Vinnie watched as I let Frank drop to the floor. He screamed in pain as he tried to stop his own bleeding.

"Donny, keep the place locked up," I said as Donny innocently popped his head out of the kitchen. "We will get this cleaned up later . . . If he's still alive, let him crawl out."

Frank's associate who'd been in the bathroom came out and looked at the scene. He looked stunned as he pulled out a gun. I didn't hesitate to shoot him in the face.

"One word, Donny, and you're dead." I shot the man a glare.

I pulled the glass out of my shoulder while I was in the shower—I didn't want to get blood everywhere. It hurt like hell. I couldn't go to the doctor after shooting a man; it would look suspicious. I hoped Prima knew how to sew. I needed stitches.

I watched the blood flow down the drain as I threw the piece of glass out of the shower. It would definitely leave a mark.

Silent Prima Donna

Gianna Marie Ferraro

prima

"Well, Mrs. DeLuca, all done." Pat smiled as she sprayed hairspray in my hair.

"Prima is fine." I tried to smile.

"Alright, Prima, this hair suits you." Pat grinned, messing with my hair slightly.

The hair was beautiful. It wasn't too different than how I normally wore it in waves, but something Pat had done made it look better than normal.

The bell on the door rang as a man walked in. It was Enzo, who I'd met at the bar earlier. He seemed like he was flustered, sweat glistening across his brow.

Enzo was short-winded as he talked. "Mrs. DeLuca, your husband told me to take you home."

He pulled out a wallet and handed a wad of cash to Pat. "He said this should cover the hair and tip." He ran a hand through his hair. "He said if he likes it, you would get more next time."

"Well, come back anytime." Pat chuckled.

"We have to hurry." Enzo messed with his tie.

I got off the chair, waving at Pat stiffly as we exited.

"Is something wrong?" I asked Enzo as he rushed me into a car.

"I'll tell you when we get you home."

Enzo being nervous made me even more worried. Was Nico hurt? Dying? Was my father okay? My mind kept racing.

When we arrived at Nico's townhouse, I rushed inside. I could hear the shower running. "Can you tell me what's going on?" My voice shook slightly.

"Nico got into a fight."

Nico came out of the bathroom, his shirt off. He wasn't necessarily fit but he wasn't heavy either. Blood was dripping from his shoulder. He held a rag on the wound, trying to stop the bleeding. "You know how to sew?"

"Yeah . . . why?" I rubbed my arm.

"I need you to sew up my shoulder."

"W-why can't you go to the hospital?"

Nico was visibly annoyed. "Just sew it up."

Enzo handed me a sewing kit as Nico sat on the couch. I dug the needle into his skin. It made me nauseous. Nico grunted before taking a swig of gin.

I hesitated but queried, "How'd this happen?"

"I got into a disagreement. You should see the other guy," he chuckled. "Guy hit me with a glass bottle. I got the glass out, at least."

"Yeah, shooting one of Ray Gallo's guys is smart." Enzo butted in. "Shooting his son was an even dumber idea."

"Shut the fuck up, smart ass. I wouldn't have if he didn't get in the way of business. We were on good terms. I'll take care of Ray, don't worry." He looked at Enzo. "Why don't you take care of the mess?"

"By good terms, you mean not talking . . ." Enzo mumbled. We watched as Enzo left, grabbing his jacket on his way out.

"He's still alive, right?" I assumed he was talking about the man who'd gotten shot.

Nico took another swig of gin. "Should be."

I tied the final knot on the stitches, then cut the thread. Nico grabbed my chin delicately.

"Don't worry, baby," he told me softly.

I hesitated to say "Are people scared of you?" .

"Most." He placed a hand on the back of my head. "I have a reputation to hold."

Nico was serene which scared me even more. Yet I wished I could be more like him in that way.

I let my gaze trail away from him.

"You make any friends today?"

"I met a few nice people at the salon."

"Your hair looks good." He smiled.

"Thanks."

He pulled me into a kiss. "I'll try not to mess it up too much," he mumbled against my lips.

CHAPTER FOUR

PRIMA

I was stirring my pot of sauce and humming "I'm Sorry" by Brenda Lee when I heard a knock on the door. I made my way toward the living room. I looked in the peephole. Two men dressed in suits were outside. I opened the door a crack.

"May I help you?" I questioned quietly.

"Hi, miss, your father home?" the one man asked.

"We are looking for Nico DeLuca," the other with a hat told me.

"That's my husband . . . "

"Oh." The first one looked flabbergasted before smiling. "I'm officer Young and this is Officer Ernest."

"He's not home right now," I told them honestly. "Should be soon."

"Can we come in and wait for him?" Officer Ernest asked.

I didn't know what to do. I'd never had to face cops before. It made my stomach ache. I was at least smart enough to know not to tell them anything, not that I knew much anyway.

I let the gentlemen in and poured them each a cup of coffee. Holding my own cup, I took a seat in the armchair across from them.

"So, Mrs. DeLuca, how long have you two been married?"

"About a month." I sipped my coffee.

"Your husband is a lucky man. He has a beautiful broad." Young smiled.

"Mrs. DeLuca, can we ask you a few questions?" Ernest cut in.

"Of course." I felt like I was going to throw up.

It was almost a miracle that Nico came in at that moment. "Prima, the sauce smells amazing." He paused and looked at the two men. "Who are you?"

Officer Ernest stood up. "I'm Officer Ernest, and this is Officer Young. We wanted to talk to you."

"They just got here, dear . . . "

"Thank you for coming, gentlemen." Nico smiled. "What can I help you with?" You could tell he had done this before.

"We were telling your wife that we had a few questions for you," Young replied.

"Prima, why don't you go check on the food."

I stirred the pot of sauce as I tried to eavesdrop on the conversation. Nico talked softly, but the cops didn't.

"Mr. DeLuca, we heard you may have gotten into a fight with Frank Gallo," one of the officers told him.

"I haven't seen him in a few months," Nico told them.

"Well, we had witnesses, and he was found dead a few days ago, along with an associate of his."

I couldn't hear what Nico said.

"We aren't blaming you, sir, just asking questions." I thought it was Young was speaking.

"You were the last person with him."

"I told you, I haven't seen him in months. I heard he came by Donny's, but I was already home with my wife by then. Ask her." Nico sounded so convincing.

"I will," Officer Young replied before I saw him enter the kitchen.

"Mrs. DeLuca, mind if I ask, where was your husband two days ago?"

I could hear Ernest talking to Nico but not what he was saying.

"He was out in the morning but was home by lunch." I lied with ease. I was used to lying for Mamma's sake.

"Did you see him when he got home?" Young questioned.

"I have the hickeys on my breasts to prove it." I looked at my sauce. Why was I being so snarky?

Young wiped his sweat off his forehead. "Fair enough—"

"Young, looks like we are wrapped up here," Ernest called from the other room.

The cops left without any further questions. I felt relieved, but I was sweating through my dress, still nervous.

"Maybe you are cut out for this." Nico grabbed my waist.

"For what?"

"Being my wife."

CHAPTER FIVE

PRIMA

Nico left me alone in the bar and all the men seemed to ignore me. There were a few older women sitting on barstools, talking amongst themselves.

I trapped my foot as I fiddled with the edge of my skirt under the table. It was the same table with the cut in it. It was right next to the back door that Nico had disappeared behind.

Enzo entered the room from the back door and gave me a shy smile. "Are you doing alright, Prima?"

"I'm waiting for Nico."

"May I sit?" Enzo asked. I nodded, and he sat across from me. "Nico's in a meeting, might be a while."

"Is it about the other day?"

"What other day?"

"When he got into a fight?"

"Oh, yeah that." He tapped his chin. "I wouldn't worry too much about it."

"Cops came yesterday."

"I heard. Nico said you did well." Enzo lit a cigar.

A moment later, a man came out yelling, with Nico close behind. I had never seen him around before.

"Don't fucking touch her or I'll fucking kill you too. Get the hell out of here!" Nico shouted.

"Watch your back, Nico. You fuck with my family, I fuck with yours." The man put a hat on before swiftly exiting.

"I take it Ray didn't like what you had to say?" Enzo questioned.

"He never does." Nico ran a hand down his face. "Take Prima home for me. Prima, I'll be home late."

"Yes sir." Enzo obliged and took me out to the car. We drove in silence for a while.

"Do you know what happened?" I kept my voice low.

"Yeah, the guy Nico shot was Ray's son, he killed him." Enzo rubbed a hand on his face. "Shit, I probably shouldn't be telling you anything."

"I won't tell." I stared at my lap.

"I know you won't." Enzo chuckled.

NICO

Ray Gallo wanted to set up a sit down after they pronounced Frank dead. He knew I was with him. He knew I did it. Did I mean to whack the kid? *I don't know, maybe I did.* He annoyed the shit out of me, always trying to buy out my businesses and saying his father had told him to. Ray knew better than to ask me for my property.

I left Prima in the front and walked into the back room. Ray was already there, waiting for me with one of my men, Rich.

Rich wasn't Italian but he was a good kid. He had blond hair and broad shoulders. He was probably one of the biggest guys that worked for me.

I sat down at the table across from Ray. "My condolences," I told him.

"Cut your shit," Ray hissed. "I know you fucking killed my son."

"If it makes you feel any better, I didn't mean to kill him." I shrugged.

I guessed that when I'd shot Frank in the leg, I hit a vital artery on accident. It wasn't the first time I'd killed a man that way.

"He was all I had left, Nico." Ray's voice was low and harsh. "After my poor wife died a few years ago, he was my only son. My legacy."

Some legacy.

"I told you I didn't mean to kill him." I kept calm.

"What if that pretty little wife of yours ended up going missing, huh?" Ray leaned in, his hands on the table.

I narrowed my gaze. "You fuck with my family, Ray, I swear."

"She's all you got, right?" He gritted his teeth. "Watch your back, Nico."

"Get the fuck out of here!" I could feel my face turn red. I couldn't stay calm anymore. He was fucking with the wrong guy.

Ray looked as if he was going to lunge at me. Rich cracked his knuckles, causing him to back down. Rich wasn't one you wanted to mess with.

Ray got out of his chair before heading out the door back, into the main part of the bar.

"Don't fucking touch her or I'll fucking kill you too. Get the hell out of here!" I shouted as I followed him out.

Gianna Marie Ferraro

prima

I watched the clock on the wall. I didn't feel like turning on the television. I felt stuck. My mind wouldn't stop racing. Why would Nico have someone killed?

Nico didn't like me going out alone, but the townhouse felt suffocating. It was nearly sunset, and I didn't plan on staying out long.

I walked along the sidewalk, my heels clicking on the pavement. The street was quieting down slightly. New York was the city that never slept, after all.

I let out a sigh before deciding to turn back. I knew Nico said he would be out late, but I didn't want him to come home to find me missing.

I noticed a white car creeping behind me as I walked. I picked up the pace. The car stopped, and two men got out. One I recognized. It was Ray who was arguing with Nico earlier at the bar. I started to walk even faster, but my heel got stuck in the crack in the sidewalk. I fell forward, losing my shoe and hitting my head on the concrete. I felt a strong hand lift me up off the ground before it covered my mouth.

I tried to let out a scream. Nothing came out. I felt something metal on my back. "Walk to the car," the man who had grabbed me whispered into my ear.

We walked with labored steps before he shoved me in the back seat. The blood from my knees got onto some of the white upholstery. The man who grabbed me got into the back seat with me. I could feel myself shaking as the car started to move.

What was going on? Did he have a gun on me? My mind was racing, but I felt like I was frozen.

He grabbed my wrists and bound them with his tie. "W-who are you?" My voice shook when I finally looked at his face. He was a younger man with dark brown hair that was almost black and brown eyes.

"Gag her, will ya?" Ray took his tie off and handed it to the man in the back seat. He tightly tied it around my mouth before pushing me down so that I couldn't be seen through the windows.

"What now, Mr. Gallo?" His voice cracked.

"I don't know, Sill, it's rare that this broad is alone. We can figure that out later. Today of all days." He chuckled. "That husband of hers can go fuck himself."

I tried to sit up, but Sill pushed me back down. "Stay down, bitch." His tone of voice seemed theatrical.

I was shaking frantically. What were they going to do with me?

Sill seemed antsy as he said, "Why are we at my place?"

"Because Nico is going to be looking for her at mine, that's why. He doesn't know who the fuck you are. Take her upstairs and clean her up. Keep her out of sight. I'll come over in the morning with a plan," Ray demanded.

"I'm going to untie you," Sill told me, "but if you run, I won't hesitate to shoot you. You got that?"

I nodded. Tears streamed down my cheeks.

He led me into a rundown apartment building, a gun to my back. He took me into an apartment on the third floor—I'd counted all the steps on the way up. There were 106 of them. The walls of the hallway were peeling paint. Random paintings adorned it.

Once inside, he locked the door, letting out a groan, before tapping himself in the face with the butt of his gun. "Oh god, that was stressful. What the fuck is Ray thinking!" He paced for a moment before turning to me. "Let's get you cleaned up." He led me to the bathroom.

The apartment looked how you would think any bachelor's would. It wasn't disgusting, but it definitely wasn't clean. It was small. From the living room, you could see the dirty dishes piled in the sink.

Once in the bathroom, Sill took a moment to pick dirty clothes off the floor, throwing them in the hallway before closing the door. He then put the toilet lid down and sat on it. He put his face in his hands.

"Go on, take a shower, clean that blood off. I'll get you a different dress after." He glanced at me.

I slipped out of my dress without hesitation. He raised a brow. "You aren't going to fight for me to leave the room or anything?"

"Plenty of men have seen me naked. What's one more?" I replied before hopping in the shower.

He looked puzzled. "What's your story, kid? How'd you end up with Nico?"

"You don't want to know about my life," I replied.

Sill didn't seem to know what to say. "I'm going to grab you a dress."

I heard the door close before turning the water on, letting the tears come out once more. I watched the blood and dirt clear from my knees. I closed my eyes. My head was pounding.

Why did they take me? From the sounds of it, they didn't even have a plan. It was pure vexation toward Nico. Sill didn't seem too thrilled by this plan of Ray's either.

I grabbed a towel and wrapped it around myself. Sill came in with a yellow dress. "It was one of my girlfriends . . . she wasn't as . . . well endowed as you, but it should work for now."

I took the dress and squeezed into it. It was too tight on me, and I couldn't zip it up all the way. I didn't know why but it made me feel more uncomfortable than being naked around him.

He grabbed my hand and led me to the living room. He set me down on the couch before going to a closet.

"I don't want to be doing this, Mrs. DeLuca." Sill sighed as he pulled out a rope. "I owe too much to disobey orders."

"I understand . . . "

"You understand?" Sill raised a brow.

I didn't respond as he tied my wrists behind my back. Or as he bound my ankles tightly. I didn't fight him. What was the use?

I was used to paying debts. I didn't know why, but I was doing my duty. Sill was doing this to pay off his own debt. Why would I fight a man for doing his duty?

"My father owed Ray a lot of money," he said, digging in a drawer, "but he died. Now *I* owe a lot of money."

"Why are you telling me this?"

"I want you to know I don't want to hurt you or keep you here." He pulled out a roll of duct tape from the drawer. He had a sorrowful look as he walked over to me. "Don't fight me, please."

"I haven't so far . . . "

"Yeah, it's weird." He tittered.

He ripped off a piece of duct tape and placed it over my mouth. I felt a tear drip down my cheek. This wasn't the first time I had been tied up like this.

Mamma got mad at me one time when I spit at a man who'd hit me—that was my first time with a man. She locked me in the closet all night, tied up just like this.

"Please don't cry, Mrs. DeLuca." His voice faltered as he closed the curtains in the apartment. "I have to follow orders." Sill walked over to a light switch. "Goodnight." Then the lights were off, and I was alone in the dark.

105

Gianna Marie Ferraro

prima

I walked into the empty living room. It was pretty late. My first thought was Prima was probably sleeping. I made my way toward the bedroom. I didn't bother turning on the light as I undressed before lying down on the bed. I went to put my arms around Prima.

She wasn't there. I patted the bed, almost like that would bring her to me. "Prima?" I called out. I checked the bathroom but the bathroom door was open and the lights were off.

I looked through the entire house. She wasn't anywhere to be seen. Maybe she was with Vinnie and forgot to tell me? He hadn't been with me tonight.

I quickly went to the phone and dialed his number. He picked up, groggy, almost like he had just woken him up. "Hello?"

"Vinnie, is Prima there?" I questioned him.

"No, why? What's wrong." He sounded more awake now.

"Well, she's not here." I rubbed my hand over my face.

"I'll be right over." He hung up quickly.

Where was she? Was she so unhappy with me that she ran away? Did she go out and get lost? Was she cheating on me?

It hit me like a brick. *Ray*. Why didn't I think of that in the first place?

I didn't think Vinnie had ever gotten to my place so fast. He was the kind of guy who was late to almost everything. Hell, I'd heard he was late to Prima's birth. If I hadn't grown up with the man, I wouldn't work with him.

When I opened the door, I noticed he was still in his green striped pajamas. His face looked flustered as he walked inside.

"You haven't seen her? Where do you think she went?" Vinnie made himself at home, sitting on the couch.

I knew he wasn't close to Prima, but she was still his daughter. It was nice to see he at least cared about her.

"Ray probably took her." I rubbed a hand over my face.

Vinnie got up and poured us both a drink. "You going to call him? Fuck him up? You know where he lives."

"I doubt he would keep her there." As much as I wanted to go to his house and kill him, I knew that wouldn't do much. It could have started a war. The most I could do was sit and wait for a phone call.

I took the drink Vinnie offered and chugged it. It was like the whisky was water. I needed to get drunk, but not so drunk that I would miss what was happening with Prima.

We waited. And waited. I had my men searching everywhere for her. Nothing. I sat in the bar toward the front entrance. I never did that. I stayed in case Ray came looking for me.

He stole something that belonged to me.

My heart had been racing since last night. I couldn't sleep. I'd sat with Vinnie for hours, trying to figure out a plan, something to do.

A nervous looking man entered the bar, a paper bag in his hand. His sweat covered the top of the bag as he crinkled it in his hand. He took in his surroundings before finally bringing his attention to me.

He walked over slowly. "Are you—" His voice cracked from nerves. "Mr. DeLuca?"

"What's it to you?" I stood up from my chair. I towered over the kid.

"This is from Mr. Gallo . . . " He hesitated but handed me the bag.

I took the bag from him, opening it. I pulled out a wad of hair. It was definitely Prima's. It smelled like her. I could feel my face turn red as I gritted my teeth.

I didn't even notice I'd put a gun to the kid's head until he was begging for his life.

"Please, Mr. DeLuca. I was told to deliver it. Nothing else." His voice was shaking.

I lowered my gun before punching him square in the eye. "Tell Ray to go fuck himself!" I shouted. "Where is she!"

"I-I don't know. He sent me to give you that."

I glared at the boy. "Get the fuck out of here."

CHAPTER SIX

prima

I didn't know if I'd slept last night, but before I knew it, it was morning and Sill was turning the lights on.

He ripped the duct tape off. It stung slightly. "Are you hungry?" he questioned.

I shook my head.

"At least drink something."

He brought over a glass of water, helping me drink it. It was lukewarm. My throat almost burned as I drank. I was parched.

He set the water on a side table when he heard a knock on the door. "Shit." He quickly put a piece of duct tape back over my mouth.

I could hear him open the door a crack. "Hello? Oh, come in, Mr. Gallo."

I stared straight forward.

"Good, she's not dead," I heard Ray say.

"Yeah . . ."

I watched both men come around to look at me.

"What the hell is she wearing?"

Sill rubbed the back of his neck. "That's all I had . . ."

"She's busting out of it. Why is her mouth taped like that? It's practically coming off. Give me the roll." Ray took the duct tape from Sill. He ripped the piece off of my mouth. It barely hurt since Sill had done such a bad job putting it on.

"How you feeling, sweetheart?" Ray patted my cheek.

I looked away from him, the smell of alcohol coming off of the older man's breath making me sick.

"Nico's looking for you. Your father too." He lifted my chin. "I can't let them have you that easy after what he did to my son"

"What did Nico do to you?" I questioned quietly even though I knew the answer.

"Well, that no good piece of shit got my son killed for one." Ray fiddled with the tape. "And I almost went ape on him right after. That man of yours was blaming *me* for how I raised him."

Ray wrapped the duct tape tightly around my mouth and around my head, going over my hair as well. It felt like I couldn't breathe.

"There, now it won't come off. Don't you worry about that pretty little head of yours." Ray looked at Sill before bringing his attention back to me. "I always say 'a life for a life,' but I'm not going to kill you . . . yet." He licked his lips and grabbed my breast tightly, causing me to yelp. I tried begging through the duct tape. I didn't know why I even tried.

"Sit down, Sill, I'll show you how a real man handles things," he demanded, pushing me down on the couch.

"Sir I—"

"Sit down," Ray interrupted.

I felt numb. The front of the dress was ripped almost completely in half. Ray sat me up.

"Do you have any scissors?" he questioned Sill, who looked as if he was going to vomit.

"Y-yeah, I do. Why?" Sill rubbed his face with his hands.

"I want something to send to Nico."

Ray took the scissors. I heard a snip and my hair got much lighter. My hair had been down the middle of my back when it wasn't curled. Now it felt as if it only reached my shoulders.

I watched as Ray collected the hair, shoving it into a paper bag. "Run this over to Nico."

"What about her?" Sill took the bag hesitantly.

"She'll be fine on her own. She's tied up enough," Ray replied, fixing his shirt before promptly exiting.

"I-I'm sorry, Mrs. DeLuca." Sill's voice shook. "I'll be back soon. Okay?"

I watched him leave before looking at my lap. It wasn't as if I could have said anything anyway. I watched as tears dripped on my dress.

Sill returned with a black eye. He kneeled in front of me as he carefully unwrapped the duct tape from around my mouth. My mouth felt mostly numb, but I could still feel a sting.

"That husband of yours can surely punch." The odd man gave me a soft smile, wrapping a blanket around my shoulders. "Are you ready to eat?"

"What happened?" I asked him.

"I went over there . . . Nico almost killed me, but thankfully, he decided to not literally shoot the messenger." Sill chuckled. "He's pretty terrifying . . . holds up to his reputation."

"I really need to use the bathroom," I told Sill. "Please." That water wanted to come out.

"Oh right, didn't think of that." He untied my ankles. "I'll make you some food, alright?"

I made my way to the bathroom, wobbling. My ankles felt numb, and my legs had fallen asleep. It was nice to finally relieve myself.

When I came out, I found that he had made me a sandwich. "I'm not much of a cook," he admitted as he placed it on his small dining table. I sat down at it, looking at the ham sandwich. It was a sad looking sandwich—one slice of ham and lettuce on white bread.

"Can you untie my hands . . . please?"

Without a word, he tied my ankle to the dining chair before uniting my hands.

NICO

I drove my car around town, looking for any sign of Prima. I even went to all the places Ray frequented. Where was he hiding? Was he messing with me?

I ended up parking in front of Ray's house. Ray lived in the suburbs, in a lavish neighborhood, away from where he worked. I stayed in the center of the neighborhood to keep control.

Not knowing what else to do, I rested my head on the steering wheel. I hadn't slept for days. The exhaustion must have been getting to me.

I opened my eyes as someone knocked on my window. It was dark outside. *Had I fallen asleep?* I looked out the window. It was Ray. I rolled down the window. I wanted to shoot him in his stupid face.

"Come inside, Nico, we need to talk," Ray told me before making his way to his front door.

I got out of my car and followed him. "Where is she?" I demanded as he unlocked his door.

"She's alive, that's all you need to know." Ray opened the door, letting me inside.

"That doesn't answer my question." I hissed."We don't touch family Ray. You know this."

"What about Frank, *my* family?"

"Frank was a made man. Prima is innocent."

"Calm down, Nico." Ray poured himself a drink.

Ray's place was smaller than mine, but it seemed to be more lavishly decorated. Everything in his place was designer and it looked gaudy. The walls were white with paintings everywhere. His couch was an ugly shade of yellow.

He sat down on his couch. "Sit down, Nico."

I stayed standing. "What do you want, Ray?"

"Six G. And she comes back safe."

Six grand? That was a shit ton of money. I had it, of course, but I didn't want to give it to him.

"I'll give you a week," Ray told me.

"Or what?" I glared at him.

"She can lose a finger or two." He smirked.

If I could have, I would've killed Ray right where he sat.

I walked down the street with my hands in my pockets, trying to decide what to do. No one had seen Prima. The only clue we had was the guy that had dropped off the bag of hair, but that led us nowhere.

I made my way down a street I used to know. It was the street I grew up on. I was a kid with big dreams of making a name for myself.

It was still run down. If I were being honest, I'd say it looked worse. I'd actually met Vinnie on this same street. We used to explore together as kids. That's how we met Zeno. Zeno was our idol.

There was still a small family restaurant across the street from my old apartment—it was called 'Papa's'.

As I walked farther, I saw the guy Ray had sent, step out of an apartment. I watched as he lit a cigarette.

I continued to watch him for a moment before returning to my car. I had to keep my mind on track. I had to find Prima.

CHAPTER SEVEN

Prima

The frigid water dripped down my face—I didn't think Sill had paid the hot water bill. It stung my skin, but it felt better than being tied up. It was the one time they let me be free. Sill sat in the bathroom with me, per Ray's orders. He stayed quiet and kept his head down, not wanting to be disrespectful. I know that because he told me. He liked to talk a lot. It was annoying and charming at the same time.

I grabbed a towel and wrapped it around myself before stepping out of the shower. Sill averted his eyes as he stood up. "I'll let you get dressed." He referred to the outfit he had laid out for me.

It was a blouse and a skirt. I had to keep the blouse unbuttoned a few buttons due to the sizing. It felt uncomfortable to be in something so small but wasn't like I had much of a choice. I wasn't as skinny as most girls.

I exited the bathroom to find Sill turning on his radio. "Ray shouldn't be here for a few hours. I can leave you untied for now. As long as you don't run."

"Okay."

I sat on the couch next to him. I could knock him out and run if I wanted. I wouldn't do that. He was just doing his job.

"Is it weird being married to an older man?" Sill asked randomly.

"Everyone asks, but I guess I don't have an answer. Why?"

Sill shrugged. "Just making conversation. I seem to do most of the talking. How'd you two meet?"

"My parents said we were in love," I replied, glancing at the radio that was softly playing "Everybody is somebody's Fool."

"Oh . . . That must suck eggs."

"Do you need to know everything about my personal life?" It was annoying how much he wanted to know.

"No. I'm sorry, I don't mean to be rude."

I didn't trust Sill, of course. He was the one keeping me hostage, after all, even if it wasn't his choice. I was still in his home.

I stood up, stretching a bit. It was probably the only time, besides when I'd showered, I was going to be able to. Sill kept an eye on me, probably making sure I didn't run to the door.

I wasn't going to run. If I was going to die here, I would die here. It was another choice I couldn't make, so why fight it?

I sat back down on the couch and took a deep breath. After a moment, the front door swung open. Sill quickly pushed me down on the couch, pinning me down. "I'm sorry," he mumbled.

"Sill, what the fuck is going on?" I heard Ray say.

"I was getting some action," he said casually as he got off me. He grabbed the rope and began to tie my wrists again.

"Good for you, thought you would die a virgin." Ray walked over to us. "Why was she untied?"

"She just got out of the shower."

"Why didn't you fuck her in the shower?"

"I didn't think of it then . . . "

"Dumbass." Ray lifted my chin. "Your husband and father are looking for you everywhere. I'm going to make sure he doesn't find you unless he pays."

"What did you ask for?" Sill asked

"Six G," Ray replied, playing with my choppy hair.

Sill looked at Ray. "You think he's going to give it?"

"He better. Let me worry about that," Ray snapped.

My head jerked as Ray slapped me across the face. "Or I'll do worse than that."

I could feel my cheek burning. I stayed quiet, trying to hold back tears.

Ray chuckled. "How did Nico end up with someone so adorable?" He grabbed my chin. "So innocent looking? Not so innocent, I hear, huh?" He let go before heading to the door. "I'll be back. Watch her." Ray exited quickly.

"What is he talking about?" Sill questioned.

I stayed quiet until Sill finally left the room.

I thought I had slept for a few hours. I didn't remember falling asleep. I woke up in a cold sweat after dreaming about Ray. If the dreams were real, I wouldn't know. Sill was in the corner of the room, messing with his gun.

He glanced at me as I sat up. "You want some water?"

"Sure."

He brought me a glass and helped me drink.

"Did Ray come back?" I questioned softly.

He shook his head. "Not yet. It's pretty late. I don't know if he will. You were out for a while."

I looked out the window. It looked like it was already dark outside. *How long was I out?*

"Who's your dad?" Sill questioned. "Ray mentioned your dad was looking for you too. Didn't know you had family around here."

"Vinnie Moreno," I replied quietly.

"Vinnie is your dad? Really? He used to drink with my dad all the time before he passed. Small world, huh?"

"Can you stop asking questions?" Why was he so interested in me?

"I'm bored, okay? It's not a walk in the park to watch you all day. It's not like you say anything or do anything interesting."

"What do you want me to do? Try to run away?"

"I'm just surprised you haven't."

"What's the point?" I admitted. "You could always let me go . . ."

"You know I can't do that. I owe Ray, and if I let you go, I'm dead and then you're dead."

He was probably right. If Ray caught me, he would probably kill me too.

We both turned when we heard the door open. Seeing Ray was a surprise.

"Did you seriously take the tape off again?" Ray grumbled.

"Sorry, sir." Sill stood up.

"Don't let it happen again." Ray made his way to the couch, sitting next to me before pulling me on his lap. "You remind me of my wife who passed, you know that? So quiet and meek." He ran a hand through my hair. "We only had one kid together. It was the only thing keeping her memory alive." He suddenly shoved me to the ground, my head hitting the floor. "Your husband took that from me!" he growled. "That's why she's here! You got that?!" He shouted at Sill. "Now, do what I tell you."

Sill helped me off the ground before taping my mouth again. My head started pounding again.

"Your husband is a fucking monster. Taking my son away." Ray paced. "I should kill you. But that would be too easy."

Gianna Marie Ferraro

CHAPTER EIGHT

PRIMA

Four days had passed, and Ray would visit once or twice a day to make sure everything was okay. And to use me. Sill would try to make small talk with me, but I ignored him most of the time.

At least Sill had started to leave the radio on for me when he went out. He didn't have a television which was fine. Listening to music was something to do.

We had both been sitting in silence until there was a knock on the door. Sill got off his chair and opened the door

When Ray entered the apartment for his daily visit, Sill seemed skittish. Ray looked me over, making sure everything was decent, I assumed.

"She eat today?" Ray questioned

"Yeah." Sill fidgeted with his sleeves.

Ray grabbed my chin and smirked. Then it faded as his face went pale. I didn't even hear the gunshot. I felt the blood splatter on my face.

Ray's lifeless body fell to the floor, a bullet hole in his head. Sill dropped the gun, shaking. My ears were ringing.

I felt stiff. I couldn't move. Ray's blood was all over my face

"I had to do it . . . Oh god, what have I done?!" He quickly ran over to me, unbinding me. "I couldn't watch him hurt you again." He hurried to grab me a towel, then wiped the blood off my face. His hands were shaking.

"I'm a dead man. They're going to kill me!" He was shaking as he cleaned me off. I couldn't move.

"We need to take you home, get you out of here." Sill helped me up.

I felt like I had run a mile, but I'd barely moved at all. Sill ended up picking me up since I was moving too slow. The effects of not walking for a few days was painful.

Gianna Marie Ferraro

I sat in the back room with Enzo and Vinnie. Enzo had fallen asleep in the corner. I didn't know why he stayed.

I was on my second pack of cigarettes. I'd stayed up all night with a whisky in my hand.

I could hear commotion from out front. "Get Nico!" I heard a man shout. Within seconds, Rich ran through the door. "Mr. DeLuca, it's Prima."

I shot out of my seat. Vinnie was close behind me as we left the room. I watched as this kid set Prima down in a chair. Vinnie ran over and placed a jacket around her.

Prima looked exhausted and pale, like she had lost some weight. Her hair was cut choppy, and the dress she wore barely fit her.

I ran over to the kid who'd brought her in and immediately slammed him against the wall. I recognized him immediately. I grabbed his collar and was about to choke him out.

But Prima yelped out, "Stop! h-he helped me."

I let go of his collar. "He did?" I brought my attention back to her.

She nodded, and Vinnie wrapped an arm around her.

"Are you hurt, baby?" I questioned, noticing the blood on her dress and the bruise on her cheek.

Prima shook her head, but there were tears in her eyes.

I slammed my fist into the wall, creating a hole right next to the kid's face. He was shaking in his boots.

"I'm going to kill Gallo," I growled.

"I already did," the kid admitted.

"You did?" I was surprised this scrawny kid would do something like that.

"I couldn't watch him do it anymore," he whispered, only loud enough for me to hear. His face almost looked guilty.

I could only assume what he'd meant by that. I gritted my teeth, but I tried to keep my cool.

"What's your name, kid?" I backed away from him, looking him up and down.

"Silvano . . . well, Sill. That's what most people call me."

I wrapped an arm around his shoulders, and he tensed up. "Why don't you wait here with my partner Vinnie? You saved his daughter, my wife. We will pay you for that. I'm going to take her home. You stay here until I get back, got it?"

"Yes, sir," he replied.

Gianna Marie Ferraro

PRIMA

I sat on the edge of the bed. I could hear Nico drawing a bath for me in the bathroom. When he came back in he kneeled in front of me and placed a hand on my cheek.

"What did they do to you?" His voice was soft yet firm.

I broke down. There wasn't much I could say. He could probably guess.

He looked at my wrists and ankles. They both had rope burn. "Let's get you in the bath, okay?"

"Okay."

The bath was warm. It felt comforting. Nico left to go talk to Sill and my father. Once out of the bath, I went around the house, making sure the front and back doors were locked.

Gianna Marie Ferraro

NICO

Sill sat across from me. He was fiddling with his fingers. You could hear him breathing as he looked at the table.

"So, Sill." I sat up in my chair. "You worked for Ray?"

"Yeah . . . " He finally brought his attention to me. "I moved back home from Wisconsin. I went to school there. My dad passed, and he owed Ray money . . . so I had to work for him."

"How did you kill Ray?" I questioned him.

"Ray forced me to keep Prima at my apartment," he admitted "I whacked him during one of his visits."

"I see." I leaned in. "The Gallo family probably isn't happy with you right now." I stared him right in the eyes. "You may have saved my wife, but you still kept her hostage at your apartment."

"I know, sir, and I'm sorry. It was against my will." Beads of sweat dripped down his forehead.

I wasn't going to kill him, but I wasn't going to let him go that easily. "You are going to work for me from now on. I'll keep you safe from the Gallo's as long as you do what I say."

There was no way in hell I would trust this kid fully. Not yet. But he'd saved my wife, so I would give him the chance to earn my trust.

CHAPTER NINE

PRIMA

Lace gloves covered the rope burns on my wrists as I entered the salon. It wasn't as crowded as last time which was a relief.

"What happened to your beautiful hair!" Pat stood up from her chair and rushed over to me.

"Fix it, please." I replied softly.

"Come on, honey, let's take a seat." Pat ushered me onto her chair. "Why are you wearing gloves, doll? It's almost a hundred outside."

"My hands get cold . . . " I was sweating.

Barbra flipped through her magazine. "She was missing for a few days, remember?"

I stayed quiet. I didn't want to think about it.

"Barb . . . " Pat shot her a glare before bringing her attention back to me. "What do you want done, doll?"

"Make it look good, I guess." I messed with my skirt. My hair was ruined, and I didn't want to look at it. Mamma loved my hair.

"Don't worry, doll, shorter hair is in style. It's not too short either. We could do a Marylin look."

I agreed before she started to cut. I'd never had short hair. Maybe it would be easier to take care of. I felt so ugly. I hoped Pat could fix it.

"So, how are things with Nico?" Barb questioned.

"Barb, don't ask a mob wife how things are with her husband."

"You know as well as I do what is said in the salon stays in the salon," Barb spat back.

"True." Pat snipped my hair more.

"Things are good, I guess. Not much I can say. We haven't been married long."

It had been a month since I had gotten married to Nico. A week of it was spent tied up at Sill's apartment. Nico seemed nice enough. Better than Ray.

"That's good, doll." Pat smiled. "You know, me and the girls like to go out on Friday nights. If your husband doesn't mind, you could come with us."

I looked at her in the mirror. "What do you do?"

"We go down to the bar down the street. Have a few drinks and get dinner. It's called Cha Cha's," Pat explained.

"I'll ask, maybe. I'll see if I can join you tonight." *I could use some friends.*

"Are you sure, sweetie? Maybe you can meet with us next week? Take a break—"

"No, I'd love to go." I needed to forget the past week. *I was going to be okay.*

Pat grabbed my shoulders excitedly and smiled. I chuckled slightly. "Great! We meet at eight."

The bell on the door rang as Enzo entered. His eyes widened when he saw me. "Wow, Mrs. DeLuca, you look like a doll. Great work, Pat."

"You know I always do, Enz." Pat winked.

The hair was definitely Marylin inspired. I had to admit it did suit me. It somehow made me feel more grown up.

I brought my attention back to Enzo and Pat. Enzo was looking at Pat like a man who was in love.

"So, you free Saturday night?" Enzo asked Pat, handing her money for doing my hair.

 "Pat, I swear if you say no again, you are going to die alone." You could hear Barb chew as she talked.

"I can't." Pat bit her lip.

"Then any other day of the week?" Enzo quired. He looked desperate. He must've been chasing her for a while.

"I'll think about it," Pat replied as she took the cape off of me.

"I'll call the salon tomorrow for an answer." Enzo grinned.

"Okay." I watched as Pat's face flushed.

I left the salon with Enzo after saying a quick goodbye. Nico didn't want me walking unaccompanied anymore.

"You and Pat are close?" I asked hesitantly, trying to break the silence.

He blushed. "I've known her since kindergarten. Her mom's sick, so she only really goes out once a week. One day, I'll get her to date me. I know she feels the same way."

"I wish you luck," I told him as we approached the bar.

"Thanks." He smiled softly.

The bar was decently empty when we got inside. Nico was sitting at a table with my father, and the bartender only had one customer. Nico whistled when he saw me. He got up and walked over to me, grabbing my waist. I flinched at his touch. That had never happened before.

NICO

"You look beautiful," I told Prima as I kissed her cheek.

"Thank you." She blushed.

I grinned. "Sill, doesn't she look pretty?"

Sill was sitting alone at the bar. "She looks nice." He smiled, finally bringing his attention to the group.

"Don't flirt with her now," I joked.

The boy chuckled nervously.

"Prima, Sill is going to be taking you where you need to go from now on." I leaned in and lowered my voice. "If anything happens, you let me know."

I had to keep an eye on him. The only reason I was trusting him with Prima was because I had Enzo following them. Enzo was now in charge of following the two everywhere. There was no way in hell I would leave Sill alone with her, but he didn't need to know that.

"Nico, we have to go soon," Vinnie told me as he nursed a drink at the table

Brought my attention to my Vinnie. "I know. Sill, can you take her home?"

"C-can I ask something first?" Prima hesitated. "Some girls from the salon are going out tonight. Can I go with them? To a bar down the street."

I placed a hand on her shoulder. "Are you sure you're okay enough? You don't need more rest? It's only been a day since you got home." I was surprised she wanted to go out. Prima looked like she could break at any second.

"I'll be okay." She gave me a slight smile.

"Okay, but Sill has to be there the whole time. Got it?" I replied firmly.

"Okay."

"Nico." Vinnie stood, "We have to go."

I gave her a kiss before leaving out the back door with Vinnie.

Bobby Gallo was sitting at the back of the restaurant as we entered. He had a sheepish grin on his face. Bobby was Ray's second cousin. I didn't think the two ever got along. Otherwise, he wouldn't have called for a meeting.

We sat across from Bobby in the booth. He smoothed out his hair before going in for a handshake. "Thank you for meeting me, gentlemen."

Bobby wasn't from around here. He sounded like he had some sort of Midwestern accent even though he grew up in Florida.

He was a shorter man, but he was buff. His gray eyes didn't look right with his brown hair. He smelled heavily of cologne. You could smell it from across the room.

"What can we do for you, Bobby?" Vinnie started.

Bobby tapped his fingers on the table as he spoke. "Our families haven't gotten along for a long time. I was thinking we could change that with me in charge."

I leaned back in my seat, glad to hear Bobby didn't want to start a war. I crossed my arms over my chest and ushered for the man to continue.

"Well, you see, I know my cousin wasn't the best at making money. But I've stumbled upon a bit of a goldmine." He leaned in. "But I will need some help."

"Go on," I told him.

"You see, I know a guy who is making snow for cheap." Bobby leaned in.

"Shut the fuck up!" I stood up. "We don't deal with that shit. Why the hell would you even bring that to me?"

Before Bobby could say anything else, we were halfway out the door.

"Who put that fat fuck in charge?" I groaned.

We didn't deal with drugs. It was a dangerous game that the cops liked to play.

Gianna Marie Ferraro

prima

I walked silently, with Sill close behind me. He let out a sigh. "I know you probably don't trust me. Don't worry, I won't risk getting killed. I told you I don't even want to be in this business."

"Ray's dead. Can't you leave?"

"I made a deal with Nico. I work for him . . . I stay alive. If I make one wrong move then I have two gangs on my ass."

"I see."

"You don't talk much, do you?" The question was blunt.

"Don't have a reason to."

"You said you are going out with friends tonight. What time should I pick you up?" Sill questioned.

"I have to be there by eight."

"How are you going to make friends if you don't talk?" Sill chuckled. When I didn't respond he said "Are you sure you want to go? You did just get home."

"Yeah, I'm sure."

I never had many friends, besides my sisters, and even then I'd never talked much. I had been called Silent Prima Donna since I could remember. Mamma's perfect number one. Perfectly silent.

We arrived at the townhouse. "I'll see you at seven fifty," I told him before leaving him on the first step.

I quickly locked the door after entering. I was shaking. Staying home was the safe option. *But no. I had been through worse. Why was this any different?*

I didn't know how to feel. A man who had helped keep me captive was now in charge of protecting me.

I let out a deep breath as I followed Sill into the bar. Sill sat alone at the bar. I smiled as I walked up to the table with Pat and two other women I didn't recognize. I had changed into an emerald green long-sleeved dress so no one could see the rope burn. I wore black stockings to cover up the wounds on my ankles. The heat made it unbearable.

"Prima! You made it!" Pat seemed tipsy already even though it was only five after eight. "This is Rosina and Winnie."

The two women waved as I sat down.

"Nice to meet you." Winnie took my hand and shook it.

"Don't worry, these ladies are nicer than Barb." Pat laughed.

Barb came from behind saying "I can hear you." I could hear Barb's bubble gum pop before seeing her. She sat down next to me. "What are you, Prima, a nun? That outfit is making me sweat."

Pat snickered. "Oh hush, Barb."

Rosina motioned to Sill at the bar. "Who's that James Dean of a man you walked in with?"

"Probably a bodyguard." Barb sipped Pat's drink.

"Kind of, yeah," I replied quietly.

"This isn't the salon, ladies, remember." Pat took her drink back from Barb. "You want something, Prima?"

"Uh, I don't know."

"Go get her a wine, Barb," Pat told her.

"Why me?" Barb scoffed.

"So you can get your own damn drink." Pat chuckled.

Barb rolled her eyes and got up. "Be right back."

I didn't notice I was spacing out until the wine glass was set in front of me. I felt nauseous.

"You okay, doll?" Pat placed a gentle hand on my shoulder.

"I-I'm fine." I averted my gaze before taking the wine.

"Heard you were gone for a while. Heard Ray's dead." Winnie stared at her glass.

"Ladies, she probably doesn't want to talk about this," Pat snapped. "I am surprised you came. You could've waited until next Friday."

I sighed before sipping my wine. It was red and bitter. I preferred sweet wine. Mamma used to make me drink her bitter wine before she put me to work.

"Don't worry. I'm okay."

"Let's change topics," Barb surprisingly said.

"You still fucking that one guy Barb?" Rosina hummed.

Barb pulled a pink lipstick out of her purse and applied it with a pocket mirror. "No, I found out the bastard was married."

Everyone but me gasped.

"What? No!" Winnie whined. "You liked him."

"Thought I did. I thought his place was too clean."

"Men can be pigs, I tell you. At least you're married, Prima. You don't have to worry about this shit."

"I guess so . . . " I messed with my sleeves under the table.

They talked so vulgarly about sex and men. It wasn't something I was used to. The way they swore so effortlessly surprised me. Most women I knew didn't. Then again, I'd mostly been around my mamma and her friends while growing up.

The room got louder the longer we sat there. The bar was covered in blue velvet with gold accents. The chairs felt uncomfortable, causing me to fidget. It felt like everything was spinning.

"Prima." I could hear Sill behind me. "Er, I mean Mrs. DeLuca. We should get going."

I looked at the time. It had been an hour. How had it been an hour? I didn't think I even took part in the conversation. At least not that I remembered.

I stood up. "It was nice to meet you all," I told them before rushing out with Sill. We got into Enzo's car, which he was borrowing to take me around.

"I noticed you looked a bit pale. Thought you might need an out," Sill told me.

"Yeah, thanks." I let out a puff of air.

"You got home yesterday. You don't need to push yourself."

"I know. I'm fine." I watched the dark street from the car window.

"I'm not fine." Sill's voice lowered. "What he did to you was not okay. Making me watch—It's okay not to be okay right now."

"I know." I continued looking out the window. "But I'm fine."

"How?" Sill's voice was soft.

"Stop pushing for answers you don't want to hear."

"Does Mr. DeLuca hurt you?"

"No." I took a deep breath. "Is life easy with him? No, but I push through because I care about him. He takes care of me"

"Then what—"

I finally raised my voice. "Sill! Stop asking questions, *please*."

He seemed shocked at my tone. "I'm sorry, I'm worried, that's all" He kept his voice low. "Are you scared of me?"

I didn't know what to say. *Was I?* He'd killed Ray, but I'd been captive in his home. It wasn't his choice, but he'd still followed Ray's orders.

"I don't know."

I didn't even notice Sill had parked the car until he spoke.

"Want me to walk you to the door at least?"

I turned my head to look at him. "Yeah, fine."

We walked up to the front door. "Mind if I use your bathroom quick?" Sill asked. "I'm sorry, I should've gone at the bar."

"It's fine, you can come in," I replied as I unlocked the door.

We walked in and I pointed him to the bathroom. I plopped on the couch and let out a breath, relieved to be home. Sill came back out a moment later. "Well, I'll see you tomorrow."

I didn't know what motivated me to say, "Do you want to stay for some coffee?"

"Your husband won't mind?" He raised a brow.

I bit my lip."He's normally out late."

Sill rubbed the back of his neck. "I guess I can stay for a bit."

I made my way to the kitchen and put a tea kettle on the stove. Then I grabbed my French press from the drawer.

I loved the smell of coffee, though the taste wasn't always my favorite. The smell of the boiling water over the coffee grains was the best smell to me.

I poured us two cups before heading back to the living room. Sill was sitting on the couch, glancing around the room.

He thanked me as I handed him his cup of coffee before taking a seat on the other side of the couch.

We sat awkwardly, staring at our coffee cups. Sill rubbed the back of his neck. "Hey, I'm sorry if I made you uncomfortable earlier."

"You're fine."

"You're a mystery to me, Mrs. DeLuca." He took a sip of coffee. "You're stronger than you look."

I took a sip of my coffee, not knowing how to respond. Sure, I had seen things, but I didn't think anyone would care.

"Part of me is curious about your past, but the other half doesn't want to know."

"You're right. You don't want to know." I finally looked at him. Sill must've moved closer to me, our thighs were almost touching. He gave me a shy smile.

He was a handsome guy. He had a round face, but his jawline was strong. His eyes were a light shade of brown, almost almond.

The front door opened suddenly, causing him to scoot away from me. Nico burst in with a grin on his face. "Prima, you're home." His eyes shifted to Sill once he got to the living room. "Why is he still here?"

"I was just leaving. I was tired, so Prima made me some coffee. Sorry, sir." Sill stood up.

"It's alright. Head home. I need you tomorrow," Nico told him. And Sill left.

Nico took Sill's place next to me, wrapping an arm around my shoulders.

"You have fun tonight?"

"Guess so. I only had one drink. How was your night?"

"Good." He got quiet for a moment. "He didn't do anything, did he?"

I shook my head. "It's like he said. I offered him coffee. I didn't want him going home tired."

"You're such a good girl, Prima." He ran a hand through my hair. "Don't let people take advantage of that."

CHAPTER TEN

pRima

It had been a month since Sill had started watching me. I got into the car and put on my sunglasses. Enzo and Sill had come to pick me up to go to lunch with Nico. They seemed oddly quiet.

I was wearing a light blue shift dress with a pink belt. I knew Nico liked this dress.

"What should I do once we drop her off?" Sill asked Enzo.

"Go home, probably. Nico will probably take her home after." Enzo gripped the steering wheel."I don't know why he needed both of us here anyways."

Sill tapped his hands on the dashboard. "Because you have a car and I don't."

Enzo groaned. "Would you stop that? It's annoying."

"Sorry." Sill put his hands on his lap.

"Why did Nico hire you?" he murmured.

"Because I saved his wife."

"But you have shit for brains."

"Don't talk to me like that!"

"I can say whatever the hell I want. I'm your superior, you know," Enzo snapped.

The two went quiet after that. They only said goodbye when we parked. I got out of the car quietly. I wondered why Enzo seemed so annoyed at Sill.

As I approached the restaurant, Nico was outside talking to someone. He smiled once he saw me, grabbing my waist. "Come on, let's go in and eat."

It was the same restaurant he'd taken me to when I first married him. We sat in the exact same spot.

"So, how was your day?" Nico asked, sipping the same brand of whisky.

I'd spent most of the day staring at the wall. I wouldn't tell him that though.

"Fine." I swirled my wine in my glass.

"Good, good . . . "

"Why haven't you touched me lately?" I asked bluntly.

Nico hadn't touched me since I got back home. He probably thought he was helping me, but it made me feel useless. It felt like that was one of my main purposes as his wife.

"What?" Nico almost spit out this drink.

"Why haven't you—"

"I heard you," he said, cutting me off "Because baby . . . I don't want to hurt you."

We arrived home late. The conversation had gone stale soon after my question, but Nico had kept me with him at the bar after lunch.

When we arrived home, Nico groaned as he picked up some mail he had stepped on that had come from our mail slot in our door.

He plopped on the couch, glancing through the mail as I got myself a glass of water. He raised a brow as he held up an envelope. "Prima, this one's for you."

I took it from him hesitantly and sat down next to him. *Stella Moreno* was written on the return address. I felt like I had been hit by a brick.

"It's from my sister."

"You two close?" Nico placed a hand on my thigh.

"I haven't seen her in about ten years."

Nico raised a brow. "That's a long time." He stood up from his seat before turning to me. "I'll leave you alone to read it. I'm going to take a shower." He gave me a slight smile before exiting.

I took a deep breath as I opened the letter.

Dear Prima,

I want to know that you are safe. I got this address after hearing your name from a friend when I got to New York. There aren't many Prima's out there. Please send a letter back to the return address as soon as you get this.

Love, your sister,

Stella.

Stella never liked to write, so I was not surprised she'd sent such a brief letter. But why had she sent me a letter? I hadn't heard from her in years. Why did she care now?

I went to the bathroom door. The shower was running. I knocked on it softly. "Nico, do you have some paper?"

"Yeah, at my desk. I'll have your letter mailed tomorrow," he shouted over the shower water.

I hurried over to the desk that was in our bedroom and opened a drawer. There was a pile of paper inside. I placed it on the desk and leafed through it, looking for a blank sheet. When I found one, I started to write my letter.

Once finished, I picked up my letter, and the papers underneath managed to fall to the floor. There were papers everywhere. As I started to clean the mess, I noticed a letter addressed to Nico.

Nico,

You can't do this to me. Prima is my pride and joy. I—

Nico ripped the letter from my hands. "You finished your letter?"

I handed him mine. "Y-yeah, sorry, I shouldn't have looked at anything."

"What did you read?" He had a towel around his waist. He put his hands on my shoulders. He was still dripping like he had rushed out of the shower.

"Why is my name in there, Nico?" I asked, biting my lip.

"Don't worry about it. Let's get to bed. We can mail your letter in the morning." Nico let go of me, and I got up. He put the letter he'd taken from me back on the desk, leaving the one I wrote on top.

I started to take my dress off to change into my pajamas. I watched as Nico finished drying himself off. He noticed me looking and smirked, grabbing my waist. I was only wearing my slip. "Whatcha looking at, doll?"

"Do you want me?" I looked away from him.

He placed a hand on my cheek tenderly, making me look at him. He frowned slightly. "I wanted to take it slow after having you back. You may be my wife, but I'm not a monster. We can have sex another time."

"I-I'm okay, really," I replied softly.

He kissed my cheek softly. "Let's go to bed."

It wasn't that I wanted to have sex. I felt like he didn't want me anymore. I needed to feel his touch. I needed him to love me.

NICO

I didn't know why I couldn't touch her yet. I wanted to, I did, but it was so hard to think about her without thinking about Ray.

I didn't have an issue with her after finding out about her past. Why was this any different? It wasn't like it was her fault Ray had kidnapped her.

I stared at the ceiling, thinking. I looked over at Prima sleeping. She looked so beautiful. Our window shade was open slightly, her skin shining in the moonlight.

I placed my hand lightly on her hip, pulling her close to me before finally drifting to sleep.

Gianna Marie Ferraro

CHAPTER ELEVEN

PRIMA

The bar was hot and sticky. It was probably the hottest day of the year. I had a glass of ice water, but the ice had already melted.

I placed the glass against my forehead. I felt nauseated and dizzy. There was no air conditioning in the bar, making the heat almost unbearable. At least we were in the shade.

It had been a week since I sent the letter out to Stella. I wondered if she was even going to come at all. It had been years since I had seen her.

Sill and Enzo came out of a back room, his shirt soaked from sweat. My father followed. They stopped in the doorway. "Prima, Nico said you can go home if you want. At least there's air there," he told me before closing the door. "Are you ready to go?" Sill hummed.

"Yeah."

Someone opened the bar door, and a rush of heat poured in. A woman entered. She was wearing blue jeans and a brown sleeveless, collared shirt that had buttons up the front, adorned with sweat and tucked into her pants. Her brown hair was pulled back into a tight ponytail.

I almost didn't recognize her.

"Stella?" I blurted out.

"Hey, little sis." She smiled warmly.

She pulled me into a hug. Then I blacked out.

NICO

"A little help here?!" I could hear a woman shouting from the other room.

"Wait, I know that voice." Vinnie stood up quickly and hurried out of the room.

We made our way to the front. A woman in pants was standing next to Enzo, who was holding Prima. Sill was fanning her with a napkin.

Women shouldn't wear pants, in my opinion. It made them look too manly. Women should be soft and feminine.

"What the hell happened?" I questioned.

"Prima passed out," Sill told us, panic in his voice.

"Stella?" Vinnie had a shocked look on his face.

"Hi, Dad." Stella gritted her teeth as Vinnie pulled her in for a hug.

"What are you doing here?" Vinnie grabbed Stella's shoulders to look at her.

"I came to see Prima," she snapped as she pulled away from him. "Prima wasn't home, so I asked around."

"Come on, let's get her home. We can talk there," I told them as I took Prima from Enzo's arms.

I didn't know much about Vinnie's older daughters. I knew one was married and in Vermont. Stella was a mystery to me. He would mention her name, but that was all.

We all stood in the kitchen after placing Prima on the couch with a wet towel on her head. We thought she had overheated.

"So, you're the husband." Stella sounded snarky as she talked.

"Yeah." I leaned on the kitchen counter.

"You're so old though." Stella wrinkled her nose.

"Stella, be nice." Vinnie rubbed his hand down his face. "You should've seen the guy your mom picked out for you."

"I did. That's why I left." Stella crossed her arms over her chest.

"Why are you here?" Vinnie questioned.

"Can't say hi to my pops and little sis?" She chuckled. "I'm passing though. I need to get to Thea before mom does . . ."

"Thea?" Vinnie questioned.

"Your granddaughter." Stella rolled her eyes.

"Oh right." Vinnie tittered. "Silvia doesn't write to me."

Stella raised a brow. "You didn't hear?"

"Hear what?"

"Silvia is in jail. She killed her husband."

They chatted about Silvia for a while. I stopped paying attention.

"I want to take Prima with me." Stella finally piqued my interest.

"No way in *hell*. She's safe here," I interrupted.

"Yeah? My friend said she was kidnapped." Stella glared at me before turning back to Vinnie. "You're a terrible person for letting her marry someone like him."

"Someone like me, huh?" I laughed. "What's that supposed to mean?"

Stella's tone was sharp as she talked. "A fucking mafioso, a Don for heaven's sake. I know what you bastards do. Putting my sister in that situation." She turned to Vinnie. "And you, you're even worse! I'm taking Prima with me! She's obviously not safe here."

Gianna Marie Ferraro

prima

My head was throbbing as I woke up on the couch. I didn't know how I'd gotten home. I sat up sluggishly. I could hear someone arguing in the kitchen.

I quietly got up, still feeling dizzy, before making my way to the kitchen. I poked my head in. Stella, Nico, and my father all stood there arguing.

"Oh yeah? I'm the bad guy? You want her to go with you?" My father raised his voice slightly. "Where were you all these years? Huh? You weren't there either. At least I'm not whoring her off like your fucking mother. I got her a man to take care of her."

"Mamma did what?" Stella's face dropped.

Of course she didn't know. Mamma had waited until Stella and Silvia were both gone before trying to make money off of me. How would she have known?

Nico brought his gaze to mine and cleared his throat. "Prima, baby, you're awake." He walked over to me, gently grabbing my waist and kissing my forehead.

"I'm going to go." My father huffed. "I'll see you later." He stormed out quickly.

"Why don't you sit back down and talk with your sister." It was more of a demand than a question.

"I have things to do." Nico patted my head before bringing his attention to Stella. "If you want, you can stay in the guest bedroom tonight."

"Thanks, I'll think about it." Stella leaned on the kitchen counter, watching Nico leave.

We sat down on the couch, not knowing what to say to each other. It was odd seeing her. Everything felt uneasy.

"How have you been?" I finally broke the ice.

"I've been good." She cleared her throat.

"It's been a while . . . since you've written to me."

She raised a brow. "I wrote to you and Mamma every week. You were the one not writing me back."

"I never got any letters," I admitted.

"Not surprised, the old bitch probably hid them from you." Stella placed her feet on the coffee table.

I don't know why Mamma wouldn't want us to talk. She probably didn't want Stella to take me with her.

Stella got quiet for a moment. "Is he treating you okay?"

"Yeah . . ."

Her voice sounded sharp. "He doesn't hit you?"

"No, he would never."

"What's on your wrists?"

I had to explain to Stella about what had happened, knowing she wouldn't let it go until I told her. Or she would blame Nico for it.

She stayed silent the entire time. Stella kept her focus on the wall as she listened closely.

"Why did you come here, Stell?" I replied to change the subject.

She leaned back into the couch casually. "To see how you were doing. I went home to see why you weren't answering. Mamma said she married you off. She wouldn't tell me to who though. She screamed about how I was dead to her. I just happened to be in New York, visiting a friend I'd met on the road, and I heard your name." She tapped her foot. "And that you were married to an old man with lots of power around here. Did Mamma choose him?"

"And Father . . . " I stared at my feet as she talked.

"You know, Prima, I was so jealous of you growing up. But now I'm not so sure. You were always Mamma's favorite. She would dress you up and give you toys. You were kind enough to share, but Mamma still wouldn't share her love with all of us. Now you're married to a man three times your age."

"He's only twice my age."

Not that that made it any better.

She scoffed. "At least you're not Silvia right now."

"What happened to Silvia?" I looked at her quickly.

"Right, you wouldn't know." She sighed. "Silvia . . . " She seemed hesitant as she took a deep breath. "She killed her husband, Prima."

"W-what? Why?"

"He was beating her—" her voice lowered "—and her baby. She's only two."

My voice shook as I questioned her, "Where is she? Silvia and the baby?"

"Well, Silvia is in jail, and Thea is in foster care for now." She looked at her feet. "I'm going up there to get Thea. Silvia wants me to. It was either me or Mamma. If I don't get her, she's stuck with Mamma. That's why I was coming this way. Then I'm probably going to settle down somewhere."

I was surprised she was going to take care of the baby. Stella had never been one to settle down and have a family. She'd always talked of adventure.

When we were young, all she'd wanted to play was pretend travelers. She used to read books about different countries and tell us about all the adventures she would have.

"What about your traveling?" I inquired.

"I've been to almost all fifty states. I can finish later," she told me, grabbing my hands. "For now, I need to take care of my family. Including you. Come with me, Prima."

I pulled my hands away. "I can't."

She looked annoyed. "And why not?"

"Stella, I have a life here now." I admitted "I think I might actually be making friends, and Nico isn't that bad."

"You really are a Prima Donna, aren't you?" She scoffed, and I could tell she was referring to me as a self-centered woman instead of an ingénue.

"Stella—"

"Are you pregnant?" she questioned bluntly.

"I-I don't know. I haven't had my period, and I don't know what to do," I told her quickly. "I have to stay here with Nico, okay?"

She raised an eyebrow. "Are you scared of him?"

I couldn't look at her. "Why wouldn't I be? You said it yourself; he's a powerful man."

Stella shook her head and stood up. "I'll stay the night here. I'm heading out in the morning. You can decide by then if you are coming with me or not."

"You left when I was fourteen. Why would I go with you now?" I snapped. "You haven't been back to see me, to check on me. Now I'm married and I'm trying to have a life. That's when you want to come back for me? After everything?"

"Prima, that's not fair—"

I cut her off. "I've been told what to do my whole life. This is one decision I want to make." Tears swelled up in my eyes. "I'm staying here."

NICO

Stella had some nerve showing up and trying to take Prima away from me. I didn't know her, and she didn't know me. I was glad Vinnie had said something before I ripped her throat out.

But would Prima go with her? She hadn't seen her sister in years. Did she trust her more than me?

I sat in the back room of the bar with Vinnie. He was a mess.

"God, I haven't seen Stella in years. She's still a little spitfire." He huffed. "She tries coming into our lives now? She knew where I lived."

I watched him pour another drink. "I don't know what to do, Nico. If Prima goes with her—"

"She won't." I slammed my fist on the table. "Prima's mine. She's not leaving anytime soon."

CHAPTER TWELVE

PRIMA

The wall looked like it started moving as I stared at it. It had been two weeks since Stella left. She'd left bright and early the next morning, not even saying goodbye.

Nico patted my head. "Sill taking you to the doctor?"

I had told Nico I felt sick and should probably see the doctor. I did feel sick. In fact, I was throwing up all the time, but I didn't think this was the stomach flu.

"Yeah, he should be here soon," I told him.

We both heard a soft knock on the door and Nico went to answer it. I got off the couch and made my way toward the door. Sill stood there awkwardly with his hands in his pockets.

Nico grabbed Sill's arm. "Take care of her. Any sign of trouble, you call, got that?"

"Of course, sir." Sill stood straight.

"Now, you two go." Nico smiled at me. "Let me know how it goes."

"Okay" I smiled weakly before I followed Sill out the door.

The waiting room smelled like strawberry candy. The ones that were filled with red goo. The room was mainly white, with blue accents on the trimming and the furniture. The floor was carpeted and gray if you looked close enough. With the white walls it made everything look dirty instead of clean. There was one painting of a fish hanging on the wall.

The fish wore a blank expression on its face. It was a blue fish that stared at nothing. I felt like that fish.

I snapped back into reality when my name was called. "Prima DeLuca."

The exam room had the same ambiance as the waiting room, but with tile floors instead of carpet. It almost made me nauseous. They had me get dressed in a hospital gown and wait on top of the examination table. I wasn't waiting long before a man walked in with a nurse.

"Mrs. DeLuca, I'm Dr. Peters."

"Hello," I replied shyly.

"So, your husband told me you have been feeling sick. What are your symptoms?"

"I've been throwing up . . . and I fainted. I also haven't had my menstrual cycle." I felt uncomfortable telling a man all of this even if he was a doctor.

"Oh I see." Dr. Peters smiled warmly. "Let's run some tests, shall we?"

I was having a baby. The worst part was that it probably wasn't even Nico's. It was most likely Ray's, given the timeline. Nico had only started having sex with me again this week, but the doctor said I was already at least two months along.

Nico took Ray's son away and now I was carrying Ray's new son. He would never see this baby as a replacement for the one he'd lost.

I felt queasy as I got into the car with Sill. "Can you take me home? Please."

"You okay, Prima? I mean Mrs. DeLuca."

"You can call me Prima. It's okay."

Sill was quiet for a moment before asking, "Are you okay?"

"I'm fine." I picked at my nail polish.

"You don't seem fine."

"Can I ask you something, Sill?"

"Of course."

"What were you and Enzo talking about the last time you both picked me up? You two don't seem to get along much."

I wanted to change the subject, and I didn't know why that moment stuck in my head, but it did. The two men seemed to be silently at each other's throats.

Sill blushed. "Uh, nothing much."

I chuckled. "Doesn't seem like nothing."

"I mentioned that I think you are a beautiful woman, and he got mad." Sill tried to focus on driving.

I felt myself getting flustered. "I see."

"Well, here we are." Sill breathed. "I'm sorry, Prima."

"It's okay." I opened the car door and said, "Have a nice day."

"W-wait. It's not okay though." Sill took a deep breath.

I closed the car door and I couldn't look at him as I listened to him speak.

"You're married and I saw Ray do terrible things to you." His gaze didn't leave the steering wheel. "I shouldn't look at you like that."

I opened the door again, leaving this time. I didn't know what to say. I'd just found out I was pregnant, and now this. I did find Sill attractive, but of course, I would never do anything.

I entered the townhouse, wanting to burst into tears, but I noticed Nico napping on the couch.

"Prima?" he called out.

"Yeah, it's me." I kicked off my heels.

He groggily sat up and yawned. "Come sit with me."

I sat down next to him, letting him wrap his arm around my shoulder. I didn't know why, but I buried my head in his shoulder. He chuckled softly. "You okay?"

There was something almost comforting about his touch. I didn't feel safe, just comfortable.

"Prima, how was the doctor?" Nico lifted my head up, his fingers cold. "You aren't dying, right?" he joked.

I didn't notice I was crying until I saw a wet mark on his shirt. He lifted my chin, making me look him in the eyes, those dark piercing eyes. They almost looked sad.

"Prima. What's wrong?" His voice was firm and low.

"I-I'm having a baby," I replied quietly.

Gianna Marie Ferraro

NICO

I pulled her into a hug. I was going to be a father. I'd never pictured myself having kids, but it felt right.

My smile faded as I looked at her sorrowful gaze. I loosened my hug. "Then why are you upset?" I pulled away gently. I watched as she picked at her nail polish.

The baby isn't mine, is it? We just started to have sex again. I got off the couch and walked over to the wall, ramming my hand into it, leaving a hole.

"That fucking bastard! That son of a bitch! Is he fucking me over from the grave?! Is that what you want, Gallo?! Make my wife miserable?! Give me a fucking bastard child?! Trying to replace your son, huh?!" My face was bright red. I held my hand that was now bloody and bruised. "Son of a bitch! That fucking jerk-off! Is this fucking God trying to punish me?!"

I brought my attention to Prima who was now shaking. I must've scared the poor thing.

"M-maybe I should go back to Mamma's," she stuttered.

I walked over to her calmly, but she turned her cheek as if I was going to hit her. I wasn't mad at her; it wasn't her fault. I scooped her up and held her close, smelling her sweet perfume. She smelled like a rose.

"I would never send you back there." I used a hushed tone. "You will stay here with me no matter what, you got that?"

"What about that baby?" She wouldn't look at me. "Should we get rid of it?"

As much as I wanted to get rid of the baby, I didn't know if I could. But it was *Ray's* baby.

"We keep the baby," I puffed, "but we don't tell the child who its father is. No one needs to know but us. Got it?"

Prima tilted her head. "What about Sill? He was there."

"I'll make sure he doesn't talk." I sighed, carrying her to the bedroom. I set her softly on the bed. "Get some rest, baby."

Gianna Marie Ferraro

prima

I laid in bed, staring at the ceiling. I sat up finally, looking at the clock on the wall. I had been lying there for at least an hour.

I brought my attention to Nico's desk. That letter was still on my mind. A lot of things were still on my mind, but I couldn't shake that letter.

I quietly got off the bed, walking over to the desk. I ploddingly opened the drawer, hoping Nico wouldn't hear it from the other room if he was still home.

I pulled the letter out before sitting by the desk.

Nico,

You can't do that to me. Prima is my pride and joy. Why would $100 a month be enough for me? You promised me $500. I expect the right amount or there will be consequences. I don't care what Vinnie and Prima told you.

Prima lies for attention all the time. I would never treat her in such a manner. I would never sell her to men. You say she has a scar on her back? That's from her falling off a tree when she was a child. Children do stupid things all the time and her childhood was nothing but joy and laughter at home until Vinnie left.

I am dealing with a lot right now and you cutting me off is not helping. I'm trying to get my granddaughter in my custody. Apparently, my daughter Silvia wants her sister, Stella, to take her. I won't allow it. I need the money to take the child to a good home.

So, please reconsider and give me the $500 a month like we agreed.

Truly,

Mamma had signed her name at the bottom. He'd paid Mamma five hundred a month for me? He'd cut her off? Well, he cut her pay at least. Of course, she would try to make me out as a liar. Why wouldn't Nico believe her? Why did he believe me?

The door to the bedroom opened gently, Nico's head peeking in. He frowned at seeing me with the letter.

"Prima. You didn't need to read that." He grabbed it from me.

I couldn't look at him. "Why did you believe me without a second thought?"

"Me and your mother go way back. And I know she's a cunt." He frowned "I've been friends with your father for a long time. I was with him through the divorce."

I never saw Nico around when I was a child, but then again, I was home all the time and my father didn't do business at home. He never even mentioned work at home. I knew Mamma would go out with him every once in a while, but that was it.

"It's weird to think I was twenty-four when you were born." Nico rubbed the back of his neck. "Your father never talked about you guys much. Just said 'my wife had another one.'" He chuckled.

My stomach twisted. I'd never thought of it that way. It was odd to think about the age gap.

I brought my attention back to the letter. "I-is she going to come back for me?"

Nico wrapped his arms around me. "I would never let her take you."

Gianna Marie Ferraro

NICO

I didn't want to worry her. That's why I never told her I cut her mother off. Cathleen was a godless whore. All the woman cared about was money and looks.

I met Cathleen on the day after her wedding to Vinnie. They met one day and got married the next. I hated her from the moment I saw her.

She kept trying to get in my pants. She dressed floozy, showing off every little bit of skin.

Her dresses were tight, and she didn't wear stockings. Her hair was always down. The makeup she wore looked gaudy. I didn't know what Vinnie saw in her. It wasn't like she had a good personality.

She used to come into the bar when Vinnie wasn't there and flirt with anyone she could. If all their kids didn't look somewhat like Vinnie, I would've thought they were all from different fathers.

Maybe she used to act the way she did to try to break from her strict southern upbringing. The woman even tried to get rid of her accent.

Something had snapped in her though, after Prima was born. She dressed properly, always wearing lace gloves. She was all of the sudden a well-behaved woman . . . mostly. But you couldn't take the bitch out of her. The day Vinnie left her was a day for celebration.

I wasn't sure why Vinnie had let her take the kids. Probably because he never saw them. He was always with me. Hell, I barely saw his kids. I may have seen each of them once.

Silent Prima Donna

CHAPTER THIRTEEN

PRIMA

"You okay, doll?" Pat inquired with concern. "You've been quiet the whole time I've been doing your nails," she tittered. "Not that you talk much anyway."

I didn't know what to say. I had so much on my mind, and I didn't want to accidentally say something I shouldn't.

"Something's up." She crossed her arms. "You can tell me, you know?"

"I'm tired, that's all." I averted my gaze.

"Probably up all night fucking Nico," Barb chimed in.

"Barb, seriously?"

"I'm okay, just didn't sleep well." I yawned.

I was telling the truth about not sleeping. I was up all night, thinking about the letter and the fact I was carrying a monster's child. My mind was still racing.

"You want me to do your makeup too? You got bags under your eyes." Pat looked genuinely concerned.

"I'm going to be having a baby," I blurted out.

Pat's expression changed from worried to ecstatic. "What? That's great, right? Does Nico know?"

"Not surprised." Barb popped her gum.

"Nico knows," was all I said.

"Is he mad or something?" Pat questioned.

"No," I lied. "He was very happy. He's excited to have a little him running around."

The salon wasn't empty. There were only a few ladies getting their hair done, but I could still hear them whisper. The news that I was pregnant was going to spread like wildfire—if Nico if Nico hadn't already said anything .

It made me green around the gills. I felt like everyone thought they knew everything about me.

NICO

I felt uneasy when everyone congratulated me. Prima was having a baby, but I wasn't the father. I had to be happy. I had to act happy.

Sill shifted uneasily as he said, "Congratulations, Mr. DeLuca."

He definitely knew. I would have to talk to him about that later.

I kept a grin on my face as Vinnie patted me on the back. "Having a kid at your age is going to be interesting." He let out a small laugh.

The kid wasn't even mine, and I had to look after it. I didn't know if I could handle that. At least Prima was young and would do most of the work like a good housewife should.

I snapped out of it when Enzo questioned, "Sir, do you want a drink to celebrate?"

"I'd love one." But not to celebrate. I had to numb the thoughts.

I sat at a table as Enzo ordered a round at the bar. "Sir I—" Sill started.

"Why don't you go pick up Prima?" I narrowed my gaze at him. "She should be done with her hair by now."

Sill obliged and headed for the door, glancing

back at me before he quietly exited. I knew he knew.

Gianna Marie Ferraro

pRiMA

The silence as I walked next to Sill was comforting.

Sill broke the silence saying "So, Nico said you're having a baby."

I kicked a rock on the sidewalk. "He told you not to tell anyone?"

I assumed he knew it wasn't Nico's. *Why would he assume anything else?*

He confirmed my suspicions by saying, "Not yet, but I'm guessing soon. Everyone was too busy celebrating. According to everyone, it's Nicos. Your dad seemed happy. Glad to have a grandchild he can actually see."

I let out a heavy sigh. "I'm not that far along. I don't know why everyone seems to care so much."

Miscarrying was also an option. I hoped to miscarry, as bad as it sounded. I would never admit it out loud.

"Well, you are having Nico's baby . . . I mean, at least people think it's his." Sill lowered his voice. "A Don's baby is a big deal. Next generation stuff."

I didn't know much about Nico's life outside of the house. I didn't want to know. I didn't think Nico would want this kid to be a part of his next generation.

Maybe it was the look on my face caused Sill to change topics. "Did Pat tell you?"

"Did Pat tell me what?" I looked at him, puzzled.

"Enzo finally got her to agree to go on a date." He chuckled. "After basically getting on his knees."

I gave him a small smile. "That's good."

Nico was standing outside the bar talking with some men. He smiled when he saw us. He grabbed my hand and pulled me close to him. "Isn't she beautiful?"

The man caressed his chin. "A real fine dame. Surprised you could snag someone like her."

Someone like me. What was that supposed to mean? Someone pretty? Too weak to say no?

"Excuse us. I need to talk to Sill," Nico told the man. Nico motioned for both of us to come.

He led us to the back room, which I had never been in. It seemed like Nico tried to keep me as far away from the business as possible.

The room was set up with some tables and chairs. A bookshelf sat in the corner. There was a poker table right in the center of the room. The walls were an odd shade of tan that almost looked yellow. The wooden floors were dark brown like the rest of the bar. The room was empty which made it feel eerie.

Nico sat down, signaling for us to follow. He huffed as he wiped a bead of sweat off his forehead. It was still quite hot outside.

NICO

I sat with Sill and Prima in the back room of the bar. He was staring at the table. Prima stayed quiet as usual.

"So, Sill." I watched Sill sweat. I took off my sports coat and hung it on the chair. "You didn't have sex with her at all, right?"

Sill blushed. "What? No—"

Prima appeared tense at the question.

"Good." I tapped my fingers on the table. "So we know who the father is, and it's not fucking me." I pulled out a pack of cigarettes.

"So, it's Ray's?" Sill replied softly.

I lit a cigarette. "If you need to know about my sex life, yeah, it's Ray's baby."

"I didn't mean to—"

"Yeah, I know. But you need to keep your mouth shut about this, got it?" I demanded. "If the word gets out, you're dead."

"I understand, sir." Sill looked me in the eyes.

I took a puff from my cigarette before saying, "Good."

Gianna Marie Ferraro

CHAPTER FOURTEEN

PRIMA

Throwing up in the toilet was part of my morning routine. I felt sick and tired all the time which meant I spent most of my time at home. As a result, it made me stir crazy.

I placed a gentle hand on my belly. It had already been five months since I found out I was pregnant. It felt like a lucid dream.

I could feel the baby kick, showing that I wasn't alone here. It was terrifying to think I was carrying a human inside me.

When I was finally feeling better, Nico took me out to dinner. People stared as I walked by. I felt like I was an attraction at a circus.

We sat down at our table next to the window. It was a quaint restaurant on the edge of the neighborhood. I believed this was the neighborhood where Sill lived. It had that family style feel to it, unlike where we typically ate our normal steak dinner.

"I used to come here all the time as a kid," Nico told me. "I used to live right there across the street." He pointed to a brick building. "Right on the top floor." He took a sip of coffee. "I used to stop here after I was done with my paper route. Until I met Zeno. He was in charge before me."

"Why are you telling me all of this?"

"My father abandoned me and my mother once he found out I wasn't his kid." Nico chuckled to himself softly. "I guess this was my way of saying I won't abandon you. It's not like this was your fault." He kept his voice low enough for only me to hear. "You've probably been lonely lately."

He was right. I was lonely. It was just me at home and occasionally the maid that came in to clean, but she didn't speak much English, so it was hard to even try to talk to her.

"If you need me, baby, I'm there." Nico grabbed my hand gently.

PART TWO

Prima and Nico

1961

CHAPTER FIFTEEN

PRIMA

I rocked my baby boy, humming to him softly. He was only a few weeks old but he was already so precious to me. It took me a long time to get used to the fact that I was going to be a mother. But I loved this baby. Still, a part of me also despised the fact he was Ray's.

I could tell that Nico was having a hard time accepting Coy as his own son. Why wouldn't he? Nico had kept to himself most days during my pregnancy. He would come home late almost every night. Nico was always working late.

He tried to take me out on dates, but he always seemed off. He was physically in the room, but his mind was elsewhere. I guessed neither of us were in this marriage for love anyway.

"Prima, I'm home." Nico popped his head into the nursery.

I smiled at him. "Are you home for the night?"

"Maybe."

"I'm putting Coy to bed. Do you want to hold him for a bit?"

Nico rubbed the back of his neck. "I'm okay."

I furrowed my brows. "Okay . . . " I softly placed the Coy in his crib. I breathed out as I looked at the sleeping child before following Nico into the other room.

"I made dinner. It should still be warm if you want some."

"I already ate." Nico sat on the couch after turning on the television.

"Okay."

I sat down on the couch a seat away from him and stared at the screen. The room felt tense. I'd barely seen Nico. I barely saw Pat or Barb either. I hadn't seen Barb since I had the baby, and Pat was with Enzo most nights.

The only person I regularly saw was Coy, and he was a baby. There wasn't much to say to a baby. I was used to being silent in the corner, but when I'd lived with Mamma, at least she'd talked to me. Nico barely said a word to me anymore.

While I was pregnant, Nico had told me that he knew I was lonely, but did nothing to change it. I was still lonely.

"Is something wrong, Prima?" I felt him wipe a tear from my cheek.

I sat up straight. "W-what?"

"Why are you crying?" He frowned.

"I-I don't know." My voice shook

"I think you do know." He placed a hand on my cheek.

I didn't even know what to say. This wasn't something I regularly talked about. I thought most men didn't care about their wife's feelings.

"I care about you, Prima," Nico told me. "You can tell me anything, okay?"

"I know I can . . . " I was almost about to say something.

"Why don't you go to bed?" Nico's eyes wandered back to the television. *Did he even care?*

NICO

I stared at the television screen after I sent Prima to bed. It was hard to look at her some days.

I got off the couch, turning off the television. I started to walk toward the bedroom when I heard the baby start to fuss.

I was going to wake up Prima, but instead, I made my way into the nursery and quietly walked up to the crib.

Coy looked so innocent, so breakable. I could have killed him at that moment, if I wanted to. I looked into his big brown eyes. They looked like Prima's eyes. I couldn't hurt him.

I scooped the small child in my arms, rocking him steadily. He started to calm down, but I felt nothing for this child.

CHAPTER SIXTEEN

PRIMA

Coy was just over a month old when Nico planned a small party to introduce everyone to the baby. I would've been happy having a few people over for dinner, but Nico insisted we go out with everyone.

Nico entered the nursery. "We have to head out soon. The party is going to start."

"I need to get my dress on quick. Can you hold him?"

He hesitated but replied, "Sure."

I handed Coy off to him before heading to the bedroom, quickly changing into a green shift dress. It didn't help cover the slight bump on my stomach, but it was what Nico wanted me to wear.

This was my first time leaving the house in weeks. I was glad to have some fresh air.

I came back to Nico. He was holding Coy awkwardly, seemingly not knowing what to do.

I took the baby from Nico and put Coy in his baby carriage. It was silent as we left, besides Coy fussing in his stroller.

Entering the restaurant made everything feel stuffy again. The room was filled with people I barely knew. I felt tense as I glanced around.

Pat was the only person I recognized. She came up with Enzo, both grinning. Pat was wearing a yellow dress, with a black belt cinching her waist where the skirt flowed out.

"Look at the little cutie." Enzo smiled at Coy in the baby carriage.

"Adorable. He has your eyes." Pat referred to me.

"Thanks," I replied.

Nico had already gone off to chat with my father, a drink in his hand.

"You doing okay, doll?" Pat questioned.

"I'll leave you two to talk." Enzo quickly walked away.

"Yeah, yeah, I'm fine." I watched my father excuse himself from the conversation with Nico before walking toward us.

"You look very—" Pat was cut off by my father.

"Let me see my grandson!" He smiled. "Can I hold him?"

"I'll talk to you later, doll." Pat patted my back before walking toward Enzo.

I acknowledged my father, nodding at him and watched him carefully scoop Coy up in his arms.

"I remember when you were this small," he told me. "I wish your mother would've let me hold you more." His eyes dimmed and his lips curled into a sad smile as he looked down at the small child.

"You never wanted to hold the girls. You were too busy drinking," a familiar voice replied from behind. The voice was proper yet firm. A slight country twang she tried to hide peaked through. "Wow, this place brings back memories."

My father placed the baby back in the carriage before we both turned to face Mamma.

She was dressed in a mint green lace dress. Her boat neckline showed off her collar bones nicely. She had a floppy hat in her hands that was the same shade of green as her dress. Her hands were covered in white lace gloves that matched her pristine white heels. Her blonde hair was done up perfectly in a French twist, her diamond earrings on full display.

The sight of Mamma made me feel uneasy. She knew I'd told Nico about my past. She was probably furious with me. I felt like that little girl who would get locked in the closet all over again.

"Get the fuck out of here, Cathleen," my father demanded.

"I heard my baby had a baby. Can't I come see my grandchild?" Mamma huffed.

"No, you sure fucking can't." Nico stepped between us.

"Nico, don't you look ravishing." Mamma chuckled. "Maybe I should've married you instead."

"You heard your husband. Get the fuck out!" Nico stepped toward her.

Mamma placed a hand on his chest, almost sexually. It made me feel queasy as she said, "Come on, Nico, I'm not married, you know that."

"Let's find a place to talk," my father suggested in a demanding tone.

"Good idea, Vinnie. Prima, come too." Nico grabbed Mamma's wrist, pulling her away. I picked up the baby before following the men and Mamma into a separate room. I could hear the people at the party murmur.

"Why are you here, Cathleen?!" my father shouted once the door was closed.

"You're rough, Nico, I like it." She licked her lips and pulled her wrist away. "And I'm here for my money."

"You don't deserve a dime," Nico hissed.

"Can't make money off of Silvia, so you come here? How low can you stoop?" my father gritted his teeth.

Mamma groaned. "Ludicrous as always, Vinnie."

"What does ludicrous mean?" I heard my father whisper to Nico who shrugged.

There was a reason I spoke plainly around these men.

Mamma continued, "I was promised five hundred a month. You heard a silly rumor. Then, all of a sudden, you give me one hundred. Now, all of a sudden, I'm cut off!"

"You know what you did." Nico narrowed his eyes. "I should've cut you off a long time ago."

"And what was it I did?" Mamma crossed her arms.

"You sold your own daughter, that's what you did!" Nico snapped.

"Who's paying for her now!" Mamma snapped back. "Silvia stopped sending me money a long time ago. I had to do something."

"Go to hell, Cathy. Get the hell out before I fucking shoot you!" My father pulled out a gun from his jacket pocket.

"You wouldn't shoot me, Vinnie." Mamma stepped toward the gun. "I can see your dick standing up. Still fancy me, huh?"

"I won't fucking hesitate. Get out." Nico's voice was firm.

"Fine. I'll leave." Mamma walked toward the door. "What's the baby's name?"

"Out!" Nico shouted.

"You want to talk to me, baby, I'll be at the Martinique New York on Broadway," she told me before exiting, a sway in her step.

"How can she afford that hotel?" my Father questioned, seemingly to no one.

"I'm going to have Enzo take you home. I'm going to call Sill and have him watch the door," Nico told me. "That bitch won't be able to get near you."

Gianna Marie Ferraro

NICO

Vinnie probably drank a full bottle of Glen Grant before finally talking to me. "That bitch still looks fantastic," Vinnie complained. "God, I want to fuck her."

"She's a monster, Vinnie, you're drunk.".

"I should've never let her take the kids. I should've been there." he buried his face in his hands.

Vinnie was rarely a sappy drunk. He was normally pretty happy. It was weird seeing him this way.

"I shouldn't have agreed to arranged marriages for the girls." He paused. "No offense, Nico."

"None taken."

I didn't want this marriage at first either. But now I've grown to appreciate Prima. Did I love her? I didn't know.

"Vinnie, let's take you home, alright?" I helped Vinnie out of his seat.

"That bitch took everything from me!" he cried.

"You're acting like an idiot," I told him, basically dragging him out the back door—there was no way we would go through the front. Everyone would give him shit for weeks.

"You're a good friend, Nico." He grabbed my shoulder.

"Let's get you home."

Gianna Marie Ferraro

prima

It was nearly midnight when Nico got home. I had stayed put on the couch, unable to sleep. Coy had fallen asleep a couple hours before. I couldn't sleep knowing Mamma was in town.

I watched Nico enter, taking off his shoes before noticing me on the couch.

Nico looked surprised that I was awake. "You okay?"

"Yeah, I'm fine." I picked at my nail polish.

Nico sighed and sat next to me. "She won't come back, I promise."

"Why did you cut her off completely? It got her out of our life," I blurted out.

Nico frowned. "It doesn't matter, Prima."

I rubbed my hand on my face. "Yes, it does."

"She kept sending me letters begging for more money. I told her if she sent one more, I would cut her off. The bitch fucking called me."

Tears started to stream down my cheeks. "I think I should talk to her."

"No," Nico replied firmly. "Why would you want to do that?"

"I-I don't know."

I didn't even know what I would say if I saw Mamma again. I barely knew what to say to her when we lived together.

He grabbed my hands and squeezed lightly. "You don't owe the bitch anything."

"Mamma was all I had for so many years. I owe her something."

Nico groaned. "She prostituted you for years, Prima." He lowered his voice. "Let the bitch die alone."

"I'll take Sill with me, or Enzo," I told him.

He let go of my hand and yelled, "I said no! Why do you want to see her so fucking bad?!"

"Because she's someone to talk to! I'm *lonely,* Nico!" I sobbed.

I could hear Coy crying from the other room.

Nico frowned. "Why didn't you tell me you were lonely? You have the baby. You have me and your dad."

I let the tears stream down my cheeks. "You're always busy, and since Coy was born, you barely talk to me. And the baby doesn't fucking talk, Nico."

I didn't swear often. I was surprised the words had come out of my mouth.

Nico let out a breath. "I'm trying my best, Prima."

"Really? It doesn't seem like you're trying at all. Maybe I should've gone with Stella." I didn't know why I had said that.

Nico narrowed his gaze. "You ungrateful bitch. I take care of you. I give you everything you need!" He grabbed my wrist." I'm trying my best to provide for you and that bastard baby! The least you can do is not see that bitch of a mother. I'm trying to keep you safe and happy. You're never fucking happy. What do I need to do, Prima?! What?!" His grip tightened on my wrist.

"N-Nico, you're hurting me." I could feel myself shaking.

Nico let go and stood up. "Stay away from Cathleen. Stay here and be safe. That's all I ask!"

"I want someone to love me," I cried out.

Nico left the room, glanced back at me for a second, and then he left the room.

Coy's cries became louder. I wiped my tears and made my way to his nursery. I scooped him up, holding him tightly in my arms. I sat in the rocking chair, crying with him.

CHAPTER SEVENTEEN

NICO

I didn't sleep a wink because of what Prima had said. *I want someone to love me.*

Did she hate her life here that much? Did she hate *me* so much she would go crawling back to her mother?

I needed to yell at her last night—it was the only way to get my point across, but hearing her cry almost broke me.

I made my way into the nursery at the break of dawn. Prima was sleeping in her rocking chair. Coy was in his crib.

I walked over to her, covering her with a blanket. "I'm sorry," I whispered,

Gianna Marie Ferraro

prima

Sill took a lengthy amount of time to drive down the street. He had finally gotten a car of his own after working for Nico. It was a gift.

"Are you sure this is a good idea, Prima?" He questioned me.

I was quiet for a moment. "I don't know . . . "

"You know I'm going against Nico's orders by taking you, right?" Sill tapped his fingers on the steering wheel. "We can turn around."

"Would you rather I go alone?" I asked him.

"No . . . " He let out a puff of air.

I was going to see my mamma. I felt like I had to see her, to talk to her. Nico obviously didn't care about me anymore, not since I had the baby. I didn't know why he cared so much about me going to see her.

I left Coy with Pat. I didn't want to risk anything by bringing him. I wanted to talk to Mamma, but I didn't know how she would act. She was an unpredictable woman.

Nico thought I was out shopping, so he gave me enough money to at least give Mamma a month's worth of money. I hoped that would keep her calm.

"Wait in the lobby," I told Sill as I exited the car.

I left him to give his keys to the valet attendant. I dawdled through the hotel doors and into the lobby. I walked over to the front desk. The man there was reading a book.

He was a shorter man with a gray mustache and black hair. He seemed completely uninterested in anything but his book.

I cleared my throat to get his attention. My voice shook slightly while I spoke. "Hi, uh, I'm looking for Cathleen Moreno." Mamma had never bothered to change her last name.

"Yes, let me look." The man barely looked up from his book before grabbing a different one. He flipped through it. "She's in room 102, on the second floor."

I thanked the man and made my way to the elevator. Once on the second floor, I walked slowly, looking for the room number. When I arrived, I took a deep breath before knocking. Fear struck me when she opened the door. Seeing her face made my stomach sink. She had more wrinkles than I remembered.

"Prima! My darling!" Mamma pulled me into a hug.

"Hi, Mamma." I reluctantly returned the hug.

"You actually came. I thought that jerk-off of a husband wouldn't let you." She pulled away, looking at me. "Look at you. You gained weight, didn't you? I guess babies will do that."

"I only had him a month ago . . . "

"I lost the baby weight right away with you and your sisters. Guess you have your father's genes." Mamma made her way to a table inside the room.

The room was larger than a normal hotel room. It had a small dining table and a large bed. There was a bottle of wine on the dining table, with two glasses, one completely empty. How did she pay for all of this?

I watched Mamma light a cigarette and puff the smoke into the air. "So, your husband let you come?"

"He doesn't know I'm here."

"Sit, Prima, you don't have to stand." Mamma motioned toward a chair.

She wore a white dress with a V-neck neckline. It was cinched at her waist with a red belt that matched her ruby earrings, necklace, and heels.

I sat down at the dining table, digging in my purse before handing her an envelope of money.

"What's this?" Mamma took it without hesitation.

"A month's worth of pay." I averted my eyes again.

"How'd you get that?" She chuckled.

"I told Nico I was going shopping."

"He can afford to give you this much money to go shopping but can't pay per our agreement?" She scoffed. Her tone changed, and I watched her swirl her wine glass with her free hand. "It seems that you told Nico my business. That's why he cut me off."

"He knew something was wrong. I didn't have much of a choice."

"You were always such a good girl. Thank you for bringing your mamma this money" Mamma smiled.

"I want you to leave, Mamma. Nico doesn't want you here." I finally looked at her.

"And do you want me here?" She scoffed.

"I don't know . . . " I looked back at my lap.

"And why doesn't he want me here? My silent Prima Donna didn't stay very silent, now did she?" I heard glass breaking, causing me to look up. Mamma had crushed the top of the wine glass with her hand. Wine and blood covering it, splattering on her perfect white dress. "You couldn't have told him you were a fucking slut?!" Mamma stood up quickly, lunging at me with the glass. I fell back on my chair, hitting my head on the wall.

"You were my angel!" she screeched.

My head started to spin as I started shaking. I could hear banging on the door, like someone was trying to break it down. I looked up at Mamma as she put the broken glass to my throat. "You were my favorite, Prima. Why would you tell those men? You love me. You love your mamma! I'll give you a cut worse than the one I did on your back!"

The door busted open as the glass started to dig into my skin. Mamma dropped the glass. I turned my attention to Sill who had broken through the door and struck her in the head with the butt of his gun.

"I'm sorry, I didn't wait in the lobby," Sill apologized as he helped me off the ground.

Tears started to pour down my cheeks. I placed a hand on the small cut on my neck. If Sill hadn't broken the door down, she could've killed me.

Sill handed me a handkerchief for the blood before quickly escorting me out of the hotel room. We didn't stop until we got outside to the valet.

"What do we tell Nico?" Sill questioned, panicked. "You have a fucking cut on your neck, for Christ's sake!"

"I'll tell him the truth." I wrapped a piece of hair around my finger. "I won't tell him you were here, okay?"

"God, Prima, you got us in deep shit there! Why did I listen to you? The old woman is mad! When your dad said she was crazy, he meant it." He continued to ramble on, but I stopped paying attention.

I didn't know what came over me. I grabbed his face and kissed him before quickly pulling away. "Uh, thank you . . ."

Sill didn't say anything as the valet pulled up with the car. We drove home in silence.

I held Coy tightly, terrified of how I was going to tell Nico when he got home. He would see the obvious bandage on my neck. At least the cut was small enough that I wouldn't need stitches, and it would heal quickly.

If Sill hadn't stepped in, I would've been dead. Maybe that's why I'd kissed him. I spent more time with Sill than with Nico. As wrong as it was, I wanted to kiss him again. I wanted him to hold me, to feel something.

I was pulled away from my thoughts when I heard the front door open. I stayed in the nursery, rocking Coy back and forth.

"Prima, are you home?" I could hear him from the living room.

"I'm in the nursery," I called out.

Nico hummed as he entered. He stopped when he noticed the bandage on my neck. He narrowed his eyes. "What happened?"

"I-I uh—" I gulped before bursting into tears, causing the baby to cry too. "I should've listened. I went to see Mamma, and she tried to kill me."

I could see Nico's face turn bright red, seething with anger. "I need to make a phone call." He gritted his teeth before leaving me to calm Coy down.

My skin crawled as I could hear him shouting into the phone from the other room. I couldn't really make out what he was saying. It sounded like he was talking to my father.

Gianna Marie Ferraro

NICO

I called Enzo as soon as I'd left the room. "Yeah, boss?" he hummed on the other end.

"I need you to take care of something for me." My voice graveled. "Take care of Cathleen for me."

"Got it." Enzo hung up the phone.

I couldn't let Cathleen live. She'd tried to kill Prima.

I picked the phone back up, calling Vinnie this time. "Do you know what that bitch tried to do?!"

"Well, hello to you too." He chuckled.

I lowered my voice. "She tried to kill her."

"What?!"

I couldn't comprehend what Vinnie was shouting after that. I thought I even heard glass break.

"Calm down, Enzo is on it." I ran a hand down my face.

"What? Nico, don't do that to her. She's a terrible woman but—"

"I don't fucking care if she's your ex-wife!" I shouted into the phone. "I'm taking care of this my way!" I hung up on him. Cathleen fucked with my life. I wasn't going to let her get away with this anymore.

Gianna Marie Ferraro

PRIMA

Nico came back to the room a few minutes later. "You won't have to worry about her anymore."

"What do you mean?" I kept my gaze on the baby.

"Don't worry about it," Nico said. Then he left without another word.

I placed the now calm baby in his crib before following Nico out. "Nico."

"What?" he snapped his head toward me.

I unzipped the back of my dress, letting it fall to the ground. His gaze wandered around my body, almost undressing me the rest of the way with his eyes. He rushed over and pulled me into a kiss. My mind wasn't thinking about Nico.

CHAPTER EIGHTEEN

PRIMA

Ever since I saw Mamma for the last time, Nico wanted to keep a closer eye on me. He started to take me out with him like he used to, this time with Coy.

I sat in the back room with Coy, who was now fussing, as I tried to ignore the conversations they were having.

Two of the men in the room, I had never seen before. One had an Irish accent and bright red hair to match. The other looked like any other man you would see on the street around here. Enzo sat with them, staying quiet for the most part.

Sill sat on the other side of the room, his eyes darting between Nico and me every few minutes. I could see Nico looking over at the baby and me every so often, getting increasingly more annoyed with the infant.

"Sill, take Prima home," he finally demanded.

"Yes, sir." Sill stood up promptly.

"Don't be so happy about it." Nico snapped. "I need you back in an hour. Got it?"

Sill stood up straight "Yes sir."

Enzo gave Sill a look before scanning the room and looking back at Nico.

The car ride home was quiet and tense. I guessed neither of us knew what to say. We kissed. Was he going to ignore that? When we stopped in front of the townhouse, I whispered, "Do you want to come in?"

"I don't know if that's a good idea, Prima." Sill gripped the steering wheel.

"I'm sorry about the other day. You can come in for some coffee."

Why was I insisting he come in? He'd said no. I should've let him say no.

"Sure, yeah, I could go for some coffee." Sill messed with his suit coat.

After I placed the sleeping infant in his crib, I made my way to the living room. Sill already had a cup of coffee in his hand and one for me on the coffee table.

"Hope you don't mind. I figured it would take a minute with the baby, and I have to be back in an hour." He rubbed the back of his neck.

"It's okay, thank you." I sat down next to the man, grabbing my cup.

Sill spoke after a moment. "Enzo saw you kiss me the other day. I guess Nico wanted him to keep an eye on me," Sill blurted out. "He said he wouldn't say anything, but if it got out, it wouldn't be good for either of us."

"I know . . . I'm sorry."

"Don't be. I've dreamed about it. I mean, uh—" Sill grew flustered.

"You dreamed about kissing me?" I chuckled. I blushed, slightly flattered.

"Well, more than that." Sill's face was red.

I could feel my face flush. "Oh, I see."

"I'm sorry, I should go. I shouldn't have said anything."

I set my coffee down and, without thinking, I kissed him softly. He pulled away and looked at me, concerned, before setting his coffee down and pulling me into a kiss.

I wrapped my legs around his waist and my arms around his shoulders. He pulled away for a moment. "W-we shouldn't do this."

"I know," I breathed out before bringing my lips to him. I grinded my hips against him before he laid me down on the couch, unbuckling his pants. I started to undo the buttons on the front of my dress, his lips against mine.

He grabbed my breast with one hand before using the other to remove my panties. I let out a gasp as I felt him go inside of me. I gripped his hair.

"Prima, I love you more than you could ever know," he whispered in my ear.

I didn't hear the front door open. He wasn't supposed to be home. Why was Nico home? Before I knew it, Sill was on the ground and Nico was ramming him in the face with his fist.

"Don't you dare touch my wife!" he shouted

He wouldn't stop punching him. You could hear Sill's head hit the ground over and over as blood spewed from his face onto the white carpet.

"N-Nico stop!" I blurted out. I tried to grab his arm. I tried to stop him.

"I knew I needed Enzo to watch you! Use my wife like that? Huh?!" He pulled a nearly unconscious Sill up by the collar, dragging him out the front door.

"Nico!" I got up, buttoning my dress back up.

"Stay here!" he shouted, shooting me a glare before slamming the door.

NICO

I saw red. I could hear Prima talk, but I couldn't process anything. I dragged Sill to my car, his pants still halfway down. I shoved him in the back seat.

"Mr. DeLuca, please! I'm sorry!" he begged.

"Shut up!" I shouted as I drove quickly.

"Don't shoot me! I'll leave town. I'll do whatever you ask."

I could hear him try to get out of the car. I pulled my gun out quickly, shooting him in the hand. I could hear the man cry in pain.

I quickly pulled up to an empty bridge. It was daylight but I didn't care. I pulled Sill out of the car. He looked as if he had been crying. His nose was black and blue, and his mouth was bleeding from my punches.

I pushed him against the railing.

"You fucking raped my wife!" I placed my gun on his forehead.

"Nico, I didn't—"

I interrupted him by planting a bullet in his head. I watched as the man fell backward into the water.

Gianna Marie Ferraro

prima

My mind was racing. What did Nico do? Where did he take Sill? My face felt sticky from tears.

Nico came home a few hours later, seemingly calmer. I stayed on the couch, bringing my attention to him as he walked by. "What did you do to him?"

"Don't worry about it, Prima, he's gone now." I could hear him go to the kitchen and open the fridge. He returned a moment later with a beer.

"What do you mean he's gone?" I stood up quickly.

"He's with your mother, sleeping with the fishes," Nico spat.

"W-what?" I felt tears spill. This was all my fault. Sill was dead because of me.

"I don't know why you're so upset. He was using you. He raped you." He placed a hand on my shoulder.

"He didn't fucking rape me, Nico!" Angry tears slid down my cheeks.

He gripped my shoulder harder. "No, he was using you. Like all the other men."

"He wasn't using me," I cried "I wanted *him* too."

Maybe if I wasn't so lonely, Sill would be alive. Nico controlled every aspect of my life. This was one thing I wanted. And now Sill was gone.

I flinched as Nico slammed his beer bottle on the ground, causing it to shatter. He picked me up by the shoulders, slamming me against the wall, a picture falling off.

"What the fuck do you mean?! You fucking wanted him?! You little whore!" He kept my shoulders firmly pressed against the wall, my feet dangling off the ground. His dark eyes stared straight into mine.

I could hear Coy start to cry in the other room. "L-let me go see the baby."

He ignored my plea to help the baby, instead picking me up and carrying me into the bedroom. "You want to be a whore, huh? Sleep with my men!" He threw me on the bed, causing me to hit my head on the headboard.

CHAPTER NINETEEN

prima

I hid in Coy's room after Nico fell asleep. I held the baby tightly as I sat in the corner sobbing. Was I a terrible person? I cheated on my husband who'd been neglecting me for months. Maybe I got what I deserved.

Nico wasn't loyal either. Throughout my pregnancy, he would come home smelling like different perfumes.

I had no clue what time it was when the nursery door creaked open. I could feel Nico's stare. I couldn't look at him.

"Prima, I'm sorry. I overreacted." He stepped in.

I kept my voice quiet. "You killed him."

Nico narrowed his gaze. "He fucked my wife. He deserved it."

"A-are you going to leave me?" I was shaking. If he kicked me out, I didn't know where I would go.

"No, I'm not." He rubbed the back of his neck. "It's not like I haven't fucked other woman."

I couldn't believe he admitted he was sleeping with other women. I never thought he would actually admit to it. Surprisingly, hearing his admission hurt, but I shouldn't have been a hypocrite.

"How long has this been going on?" Nico questioned.

I tried to keep calm. "That was the first time."

"Good." He crouched down on the floor to get more to my level. "You fuck anyone but me ever again, there will be trouble. Got it?"

I looked at the sleeping baby in my arms. He was so peaceful.

"Why did you do it?" he questioned me.

"The same reason as you, I suppose. I was lonely," I admitted.

I didn't love Sill. He was just a man who gave me attention. He cared about me. I'd like to think I cared about him too.

He ran a hand through my hair "I'll try to do better, I promise."

"Promise me you won't cheat again."

"Prima, I'm a man with needs. I can't—"

"Promise me. I'm right here, Nico. I'm in your home. You need me, I'm here."

"Fine. I promise." Nico stuck his hands in his pockets. "Go to bed, Prima."

Why was I so desperate to have Nico to myself? Maybe so I wouldn't feel as lonely. So I'd feel wanted.

CHAPTER TWENTY

Prima

It had been a week since Sill was killed. With him gone, Enzo was back to taking me around. That made Enzo happy since he got to see Pat more often.

Sill was constantly on my mind, but I tried not to show it. It was my fault he was dead, after all. I shouldn't have made a decision for myself. Every time I did, someone ended up hurt.

"I'll pick you up in two hours. Nico wants you at dinner by seven," Enzo told me as we entered the salon.

"Will I see you for dinner?" Pat asked Enzo, giving him a wink.

"Maybe you will." He walked over to her, grabbing her waist and giving her a kiss.

"Now go, I have to work." Pat giggled, pushing him off.

I wanted the love Pat and Enzo had. It wasn't lust. It was love. It was so pure. They always seemed so happy.

I sat down in Pat's chair, watching the couple say goodbye before Enzo left. Pat smiled as she turned her attention toward me. "The usual?"

I nodded.

"Where's the baby?" Pat hummed as she started to mess with my hair.

I looked at myself in the mirror. "We have someone watching him tonight. It feels weird leaving him alone with a stranger. Well, Nico knows her."

"I couldn't imagine." Pat continued to hum as she put a roller in my hair.

"Why is Enzo dragging you around now?" Barb popped her gum. "What happened to what's his face?"

"He's gone now," I replied softly.

"Oh," was all Pat said.

I would've thought Pat would know. I guess Enzo didn't share everything with her.

"So, Nico's taking you to dinner?" Pat smiled, changing the subject. "Been a while, huh?"

"Yeah, it's been a while. He's taking me somewhere new, I guess. He seemed excited."

"Are you excited?" Pat questioned.

"Yeah, I guess so." I didn't know how I felt. I felt numb.

Sill was all I could think about. Why did I want Sill so bad? Was I really so lonely to cost a man his life? I should've begged Nico for more attention. *Sill would still be here today if I did.*

"Are you going to join us on Friday?" Barb questioned.

"I don't think so . . . " I shifted my gaze.

I could hear Barb chewing her gum. "Don't be a buzzkill, Prima."

"I understand with the baby. Some people need to understand that." Pat glared at Barb.

Barb scoffed and went back to her magazine.

I wasn't used to having friends or being invited to things. It was odd to have a group of women that actually want to spend time with me.

I wasn't ready to leave Coy alone with Nico. I didn't know if I could trust him with Ray's baby.

Gianna Marie Ferraro

NICO

I was overwhelmed by the jewelry behind the glass case. I felt like I had to get Prima something. I didn't keep my part of the deal last night. As soon as I'd left, I found a woman and fucked her.

I didn't know what type of jewelry Prima liked. Aside from earrings, she rarely wore any.

A bracelet caught my eye. It was gold. She wore gold, right? "How much is that one there?" I questioned the jeweler.

"Two hundred," he told me. "It's genuine gold."

I looked at the clock. "Shit, I'm late. Yeah, I'll take it. Make it snappy."

"For the wife?" the jewelry questioned as he wrapped up the bracelet.

"Yeah," I told him as I pulled out a wad of cash. "Wanted to get her something special."

"Very good choice, sir." He smiled.

Once he finished wrapping up the bracelet, he took the money and I rushed out the door.

Gianna Marie Ferraro

prima

Nico was late to dinner for once. I tapped my foot as I sipped a glass of sweet wine, trying to calm myself down. It had been so long since we had gone on a date. What would I even say to him?

The restaurant looked even more expensive than usual. I felt out of place. I was dressed decent, of course, but I still felt odd. He had taken me to so many lavish places, but each of them made me feel sick.

I was wearing a lavender dress with a square neckline. I had a plain silver necklace with a single pearl that I had picked out for myself.

The room had blue curtains along two of the walls, making the white wall stand out. The floor was bright white marble, with specks of silver scattered throughout. The tables were all adorned with light blue tablecloths, matching the curtains.

Nico entered with a grin on his face. "Prima, you look beautiful." He bent down to kiss my cheek before taking a seat.

"Thank you." I took another sip of my wine.

I watched Nico pour himself a glass before pulling something out of his pocket. "I got you something. That's why I was late."

He handed me a black velvet box. I took it gently, opening it. It was a beautiful gold bracelet with diamonds scattered on it. It wasn't something I would normally pick, but I couldn't complain.

"It's beautiful, thank you." I smiled at him as he put it on me.

I looked at the bracelet on my wrist for a moment. It looked expensive. "It's real gold and diamonds so be careful," Nico told me, confirming my suspicion.

"Is there an occasion for this?" I questioned.

Nico smiled. "I wanted to get you something special."

The waiter came over and took our order before I brought my attention back to my wine. I wasn't much of a drinker. I could feel the alcohol affecting me already.

"How was Coy when you left?" Nico swirled his drink.

"Crying. Fran seemed nice, though." I referred to the babysitter.

Nico smiled and grabbed my hand. "She babysits almost every kid and baby in the neighborhood. He should be fine."

"Okay" I finished my glass before pouring another. Leaving Coy with a stranger still made me nervous.

"I think we should go on vacation sometime," Nico told me.

"Yeah? Where?"

"Don't know yet. I have some business to do in Philly. Maybe we could pop down there. Otherwise, I'll send Enzo."

"Yeah, maybe."

We never went on the honeymoon he'd promised. It was always business with him.

Gianna Marie Ferraro

NICO

Dinner went on, mostly with me doing the talking. Prima nearly finished the bottle of wine by herself. She was stumbling as we left the restaurant.

"I don't think I've ever seen you drink that much." I chuckled as she grabbed his arm for support.

"That's because I don't." Prima hiccupped.

"Let's get you home and get you some water, okay?" I smiled.

"Yeah, Nico, make that choice for me," she slurred as I helped her in the car.

"What are you talking about?" I questioned as I got in the driver's seat.

"All the decisions I make end up badly," she told me, leaning on the window. "So why should I make any?" She was definitely drunk. She was probably drunk by glass two.

"Prima, let's get you home," I replied calmly.

"Come on, Nico." She placed a hand on my leg. "I don't get to choose anything, and you know that. Who to marry, who to fuck, who I have a fucking child with." She laughed.

I stayed quiet. Drunk Prima was not something I was used to seeing, and frankly, she was going crazy.

Once we got home, I pulled her out of the car and picked her up.

"You think this bracelet is going to make up for you neglecting me these past few months?" She chuckled as I carried her inside. "I don't even fucking wear gold."

Of course she didn't.

Fran was sitting on the couch watching the television. "Fran, you can leave now." She looked as uncomfortable as I felt

"Yeah, Fran, has he fucked you too?" She laughed.

"The baby is sleeping . . . So you know." Fran stood up and quickly left.

I took Prima to the bedroom and set her on the bed.

"What the fuck is your problem?"

"No problem at all." She kicked off her heels.

Something had to be wrong. "Get ready for bed. I'll get you some water." I started to leave the room. "So you know, Prima, I know that you didn't choose to marry me, but I don't regret my decision one bit."

pRiMA

I threw up for at least an hour after waking up. I leaned against the wall, the cool tile on the floor cooling me down as I slid down to the floor. When I looked up, Nico was standing in the doorway holding Coy, bouncing him.

"Feeling better?" he questioned.

"I'm sorry, Nico . . . "

"I know."

"I didn't mean—"

"I know you meant what you said. It's okay, I liked when you finally spoke up for yourself. It was frustrating but kind of sexy."

"I don't regret marrying you either," I told Nico, getting off the floor. I might not have remembered everything from last night, but I did remember him saying that.

He gave me a slight smile. "I'm glad."

PART THREE

Prima and Nico

1962

Gianna Marie Ferraro

CHAPTER TWENTY-ONE

prima

I hated going to the horse races. Nico wasn't much of a gambler, but he would indulge himself every once in a while and force me to go with him. He called me his good luck charm since he always won when I was with him.

There were hundreds of men and a few women all crowded into the stands of the horse race track. The shouting from the angry gamblers made me dizzy. It always seemed to be ninety degrees outside, the sun beating down, and smelling like sweat whenever we came here. This sunny day in July was no different. At least he let me stay home during the winter months.

It seemed to be the only time he wanted to spend time with me. We would go to dinner maybe once a month and it was normally after the horse races.

One good thing about today though was that Pat came with Enzo. The two had been engaged for a few months now.

"How's Coy?" Pat questioned. "He with Fran?"

"Yeah." I let out a puff of air. I was feeling nauseous "He runs . . . a lot now. Really fast. So it's nice to have a break." I chuckled.

Pat gave me a smile. "He's a little ankle biter, isn't he?" She laughed. "How old is he now?"

"He turned a year old in May," I told her.

"Fucking hell!" Nico interrupted. "Come on, you lazy horse, move!" he shouted. He was betting on a horse named Nicknack that was number fourteen. It was a beautiful black stallion he often betted on.

Nico grabbed my hand tightly as we watched the horse somehow pass number six, then seven, then thirteen. He was in the lead. Nico kissed me as soon as Nicknack crossed the finish line. I could taste the sweat on his lips. I felt sick from the smell.

"I knew you were my good luck charm," Nico snickered. "Just can't let go of you." He gave my hand a peck.

I felt like I was going to throw up. "I need to run to the powder room," I told Nico.

"Want me to come with, doll?" Pat questioned.

"please."

I wiggled my way down the aisle of chairs, Pat following close behind.

When we arrived at the bathroom, I immediately ran into a stall, throwing up. "God, that smell."

I could feel Pat pulling my hair back as I threw up more. Once done, she helped me off the ground and onto a chair that was in the corner.

She felt my head with the back of her hand. "Well, you don't have a fever. Was the heat too much?"

"I'm six months pregnant, Pat." I let out a heavy sigh. After the last pregnancy, I was too scared to tell anyone, especially Nico. I wasn't sure why because, this time, it was his.

Nico didn't notice the weight gain. No one did. I wore A-line skirts and dresses. I only now started to show more. Nico hadn't touched me in over a month, so why would he notice?

"That's great, Prima!" Pat exclaimed.

"Glad you think so. You're the first to know . . ."

"Nico doesn't know yet?" Pat questioned.

I shook my head. Pat didn't know about Ray being Coy's father. She would never understand why I hid it this long.

"How long have you known?"

"Three months."

"Why haven't you told anyone?" Pat looked a little bewildered.

"I don't know . . ."

I didn't know how to even begin to explain. I couldn't tell her about Coy's father, for Nico's sake.

"Doll, you know you can tell me anything, right?"

"I know." I went quiet after that.

"Let's go back out there, okay?" Pat let out a heavy sigh.

Gianna Marie Ferraro

NICO

We went to the same restaurant we always did after the races. A small pasta shop called 'Tuttos.' I watched as Prima picked at her meatballs. I was already halfway done with my food, and she'd barely touched hers.

"Something wrong?" I questioned nonchalantly as I shoved a meatball in my mouth.

"I'm pregnant," she blurted out.

I almost choked on my meatball. "What?"

It didn't feel real. Was she telling the truth? Why would she lie about that? Was the kid even mine? My mind was racing.

"It's yours, don't worry." She kept her voice low as she continued to pick at her food.

"How long have you known?"

"A few months . . . "

My heart pounded. I felt a combination of happiness and disgust at the same time.

"How far along are you?"

"Six months." She answered so bluntly, it was almost like she had no emotion.

"Why didn't you tell me?" I could hear the hurt in my own voice. "Are you scared of me?"

I watched a few tears start to drip down her cheeks. "I'm not ready for another baby, okay?"

I watched her rush out of her chair and toward the bathroom. *Was I happy?* I couldn't tell.

prima

The car ride home was silent. When we got home, we both sat in the car for a moment, not knowing what to say to each other.

"It's my kid?" Nico questioned.

"Yes, of course it is." I had barely left the house in months and never alone.

He grabbed my hand, causing me to bring my attention to his face. He had a wide grin. "I'm going to be a father."

I didn't know why that sentence stung so bad. Nico was a father to Coy. *Did he still not see him as his son?*

CHAPTER TWENTY-TWO

prima

My little girl slept peacefully in my arms as I rocked in my rocking chair. We had decided to name her Audrey. She was the most beautiful baby girl I had ever seen in my life.

I chuckled as I brought my attention to Coy who had grabbed my leg. He giggled before looking at the small baby in my arms.

Coy hadn't had much of a reaction toward the baby since she was born. He would acknowledge Audrey but never tried to play or talk to her.

I could hear the front door open. Coy immediately ran to meet Nico. Nico came in with a grin, holding the small child in his arms.

"How was your day?" I questioned him.

"Good," he puffed. "Lots of work to do." I watched him set Coy on the ground. I didn't push further.

Lately, the more I tried to talk to Nico, the more annoyed he seemed with me. It seemed the longer he was home, the sooner he wanted to leave. He would leave me alone with the kids more often than not. I didn't know how to talk to him anymore.

NICO

I hated being home. The kids were always so nosy. Coy looked more and more like Ray every day. I couldn't stand to look at him. I acted Happy for Prima's sake. It was breaking me down.

I was happy to have a child of my own. But I wished Audrey was a boy. I wished Coy was mine.

PART FOUR

Prima and Nico

1973

CHAPTER TWENTY-THREE

prima

Elton John's song "Empty Sky" played on the radio softly as I finished smearing peanut butter on the peanut butter and jelly sandwich. I almost dropped my butter knife as Audrey grabbed my leg.

Both kids were a handful, but Audery was sensitive and Coy was a ball of energy. Coy was almost twelve and Audrey was almost ten.

"Mommy, can I have two sandwiches for lunch?" the little blonde tilted her head, looking up at me, keeping her arms wrapped around my legs.

Audrey had Nico's dark eyes and my golden hair. Coy was a different story. He mainly looked like me, except for his nose and the fact that his hair was light brown, probably like Ray's before the gray hair. I told everyone he got it from my Mamma's side.

"Baby, you barely finish one." I chuckled. "You need to finish getting ready. Put your shoes on."

"Mom, can I have two sandwiches?" Coy questioned entering the kitchen.

"I already made it," I told him.

"How come he gets two!" Audrey pouted, letting go of my leg.

"Because he can eat more than you. I'll tell you what, you finish the whole thing, I'll make you two tomorrow," I told her.

I tensed as Nico entered the kitchen, groaning. He was wearing his red striped robe. "Could you three be any louder?"

"Sorry, Daddy!" Audrey replied, attaching herself to his leg.

"Go get ready for school, princess. I'm going back to bed." Nico kissed the top of her head before detaching her from his leg.

Nico smiled at me before heading back to the bedroom. His hair had started to gray, and he had a few wrinkles around his eyes, starting to show his age. He was only fifty-six, but I could only assume his job was stressful, along with taking care of two kids.

I still barely saw him. He was always at the bar or out on the town. He didn't get home until at least 2:00 a.m. last night. I dealt with it like I was expected to.

"Is uncle Enzo taking us to school again?" Coy questioned.

"He should be here any minute. I'm coming with you today. He's taking me shopping," I told them as I finished putting their lunches in paper bags.

Enzo still took me around. He now also had the job of taking my kids to school when he could. I would walk the kids to school most days alone. But I had a feeling someone was watching us from a distance.

"Are you shopping for my birthday?" Coy questioned excitedly.

"Maybe." I winked, handing the two their lunches.

I rushed the two out the door when I heard Enzo honk. I smoothed out my skirt as I got in the front seat. Nico insisted that I wear skirts and dresses when I went out, even if pants were more in style.

"Uncle Enzo! Are you and Aunt Pat still coming to my birthday party Saturday?" Coy queried.

"I wouldn't miss it for the world," Enzo replied with a smile.

"Mom, can I go over to Mary's after school?" Audrey asked.

"Honey, Grandpa is coming for dinner, remember?" I told her.

"Oh, right." Audery giggled.

Once we got to the school, I helped the kids out of the car, giving them each a kiss before sending them on their way.

I watched as the other moms whispered to each other before getting back in the car. I leaned back a bit in my seat. I closed my eyes for a moment.

I needed a moment of silence.

"Coy is going to be twelve now?" Enzo asked.

I opened my eyes and brought my attention to Enzo. "Yeah, he's growing like a weed."

"He's starting to look a lot like Ray . . . " His voice faltered as he spoke.

I frowned. I figured that Enzo knew. Even though my father was Nico's right hand man, it seemed Enzo had the inside scoop on his personal life.

I kept my voice low. "Don't say that, please."

"Sorry . . . it's just people might start to notice," Enzo admitted.

"Ray's been dead for years," I snapped at him. "I doubt they will."

"Prima, people talk."

I stayed quiet, not knowing what to say. The last thing I wanted was for people to know the truth, for Coy's sake.

"Where did you want to shop?" Enzo replied, changing the subject.

"Any toy store will do."

"Maybe Jenkins toys?" Enzo questioned as he turned the wheel.

Jenkins was a small toy store in our neighborhood. It was quaint and my kids loved going there.

"That sounds great, thanks." I smiled.

Enzo let me out at the front of the store and said, "I'll be back in twenty but take your time. I have to take care of something."

I watched him drive off.

I walked into the store and started to look around for any toy I thought Coy might like. I turned down an aisle and almost ran into a woman. It was Mary's mom, Marie.

She was a stout woman with dyed blonde hair. Her roots were turning gray. She wore a green blouse with brown slacks.

"Sorry," I apologized as I tried to get around her.

"Prima! How are you doing?" Marie questioned, her voice annoyingly loud.

"I'm good, thanks." I gave her a fake smile.

"What brings you here?" she queried.

I let out a breath. "Just looking for a gift for my son."

"I see . . ."

"Well, I'll see you later," I told her as I rushed off.

"I'll see you at the party Saturday!" she called out.

It's not that I didn't like Marie. She was just very . . . loud. Her daughter was Audrey's friend, so I did see her quite often.

Once I found the perfect toy, a box of small army men, I made my way back to the car. Enzo was tapping his fingers on the steering wheel. I noticed little spots of blood on his shirt.

"You might want to change," I told him as I got in the car.

"Yeah, I know." Enzo started to drive.

"How's Pat doing?"

"Good, lots of morning sickness though. Not as bad as you were, thank God. She's still able to work," he told me. "She's eating everything too."

I chuckled. "Well, you do have three mouths to feed now.

"Yeah, I had to ask Nico for more jobs. Thankfully, he agreed," Enzo admitted.

"You work hard enough," I shrugged.

"Yeah, and I didn't fuck his wife." Enzo went quiet for a moment in my silence, then said, "Sorry."

We stayed quiet the rest of the ride.

I walked alone to pick up the kids. I watched the two children run up to me, I kneeled down, pulling them into a tight hug. "How was school?"

"Good! Mrs. Richards wants to talk to you though," Coy told me.

"About what?" I could see her waiting by the door.

"I don't know."

"Why don't you two play on the playground with the other kids?" I told them as Mrs. Richards started to walk over to me.

Mrs. Richards was a stern looking woman. Her hair was always in a tight bun and her black rimmed glasses almost looked too big for her face. She normally wore a pantsuit that was a size too big.

"Mrs. DeLuca, mind if I have a word?" she questioned, pulling me to the side as my kids ran off to play.

"Is there a problem?" I replied.

"Of sorts, yes." She pushed up her glasses.

I looked at the children before bringing my attention back to her. "What can I help you with?"

She cleared her throat. "Well, your son gave out birthday cards earlier this week and I have some . . . concerns from the parents."

"It's bowling. I don't know what there is to be concerned about." I chuckled nervously.

"Well, there are rumors about your husband's . . . occupation." She cleared her throat. "And several of the parents in our school have expressed concerns. So don't expect many children to attend. I'm an educator so I don't judge. But some of the parents don't want your kids around theirs. But as they are children, I did defend them. It's not your children's fault, after all. "

I was shocked. It had never been a problem before with the kids, at least not that I'd noticed.

"Well, have a nice day, Mrs. Richards." I gritted my teeth. "Kids! Let's go!" I called out.

"Five more minutes!" Coy begged.

"Come on, Grandpa will be there soon, and we need to get you cleaned up." I called out.

I held both children's hands as we walked. My mind was racing. I didn't want my kids to grow up lonely like I had. We put them in a private school so they could get away from Nico's world. At least that's why I wanted them there.

"Mamma, Ben said that Dad is a bad man. Is that true?" Coy looked up at me.

I stopped for a moment, not really knowing what to say. What were the parents telling their kids, and why hadn't it been an issue until now? Did they just find out who my husband was? We had the same last name, for heaven's sake.

"Your father is a good man. He's not perfect, but he's a good man," I told them as we continued walking.

"Ben said that his dad said that he can't play with me anymore," Coy replied sadly.

My chest ached as tears threatened to spill, but I kept a stern expression. "Well, that's Ben's loss. You can make other friends."

"Ben was my only friend . . . " I heard Coy murmur.

Once we arrived at the house, I rushed the kids off to get showered and ready for dinner. I placed a hand over my mouth, letting out a small sob as I walked into the kitchen. I took a deep breath as I got some vegetables out of the fridge, getting ready to cook. I heard the front door open, and Nico walked into the kitchen.

"How was your day?" he questioned. "You look tired."

"It was fine," I replied as I started to chop some vegetables.

"Doesn't seem fine." He placed a hand on my shoulder.

My face was probably puffy.

"Coy's teacher came up to me today and told me that not many of the kids are coming to his party," I told him with a frown.

He raised a brow. "Why's that?"

"They found out something . . . " I kept my voice quiet.

"What did they find out?"

"That you're his father." I let out a breath.

"See, this is why we should've put our kids in public school. Those fuckers don't understand anything." Nico went into the fridge to grab a beer.

Nico was the one that insisted that the kids go to private school. He wanted them to have a good education. I stayed silent about the matter.

"What are you making for dinner?" Nico questioned.

"Spaghetti and sausage," I replied as I went into our fridge to grab a jar of sauce I had made the day before.

"Your dad is coming. You aren't making anything better?" Nico huffed.

I let out a sigh. "It's his favorite, and I've been too busy planning this party that apparently no one is going to, besides Marie and her daughter, Mary."

Nico groaned. "Marie's a bitch. Why would you invite her?"

"Because Audrey is friends with Mary."

"Doesn't make her less of a bitch." Nico took a swig of his beer.

"Can I talk to you about something, Nico?"

He looked at me for a moment, waiting for me to say something.

I cleared my throat. "Enzo mentioned that Coy looks a lot like Ray . . . "

"Don't talk about that man in this house. You know not to talk about him here." He slammed his beer on the counter, causing me to jump. "We made a deal. We don't say shit."

"Who's Ray?" I heard a small voice ask from the entrance of the kitchen. We both turned to see Coy. We hadn't heard him come in.

"No one, sweetie. Why don't you get cleaned up for dinner," I told Coy calmly.

"Okay . . . " Coy replied, looking at Nico who looked clearly annoyed.

Nico turned to me once Coy left. "See, this is why we don't say anything when the kids are home."

"I-I'm sorry, I didn't know he was there."

"Make dinner. Your dad will be here soon." Nico downed his beer before throwing it in the trash.

Nico had started to drink more each year since Coy was born. I wasn't sure whether it was to deal with stress from work or if Coy was the issue. I hated to think that way.

My father opened the front door with a huge grin on his face. "Where's my little ankle biters?"

Both kids immediately grabbed onto his legs. "Grandpa!" they exclaimed.

"Kids! I'm too old for this." My father laughed, shaking them off.

"Vinnie, how's the new girlfriend?" Nico chuckled, shaking his hand.

"She left me already, oh well," he chuckled.

I still didn't know much about my father's life. We had him over every Wednesday for dinner, but he mostly talked to Nico and the kids. Sure, I would see him at the bar, but other than that, we were basically strangers.

We all sat down to eat, Nico at the head of the table and both my kids next to me. My father sat across from Nico.

"So, Coy, are you excited for your party?" my father questioned.

"Of course! Are you going to be there, Grandpa?"

"I wouldn't miss it for the world." He smiled.

Although my father wasn't in my life much, he at least tried to be there for the kids. Dinner once a week was at least something.

"Grandpa, where's Grandma?" Audrey piped up. "All my other friends have a grandma."

"Eat your food, Audrey," I told her.

"She died a long time ago, sweetheart," my father replied. "She passed from cancer. May she rest in peace."

It was probably better to lie to them than tell them the truth. I stayed quiet about the whole situation, swirling my pasta around my fork.

"So, Prima." My father wiped his mouth with a napkin. "What have you been up to?"

I was taken aback by the question. He rarely asked me anything. "Oh, mainly planning the party."

"Should be fun then." He smiled.

I brought my attention back to my fork. I'd made the sauce too salty.

"You should come over. It's been a while," my father said, trying to get my attention again.

I looked at him. "Yeah, that would be nice."

Father smiled. "You can come over on Monday when the kids are in school. That sound good?"

"Yeah, that should work."

I realized I hadn't brought my full attention to my father in a long time. He looked so old. His hair was fully gray now and he had wrinkles on his forehead. He seemed to have gained some weight too.

My father brought his attention back to Nico. "So, are you two planning on having any more kids?"

Nico nearly choked on his sausage. "No, I'm too fucking old." He laughed.

"How old are you, Papa?" Audrey questioned.

"Old enough to not have any more kids." Nico chuckled and ruffled her hair.

After dessert, Coy asked, "Dad, can we go play outside?"

Nico wiped his mouth and let out a heavy sigh. "Yeah, but be back before dark, got it?"

"Thanks, Pops!" Coy replied as he and Audrey flew out of their chairs and out the door.

My father chuckled. "Man, to be that young again."

"You got that right." Nico chuckled. "Those two love to play."

"They're kids, you gotta let them."

"True. Prima, why don't you grab the wine?" Nico hummed.

NICO

Prima felt tense as I put my arms around her from behind. She set down the dish she rinsed and let out a long sigh.

"Kids are in bed," I told him, placing a kiss on her neck. "Dinner was good."

"Thanks," she replied, drying off the dish.

"I'm going to get ready for bed." I let go of her waist.

"You aren't going out tonight?" she questioned.

I normally went out every night, mainly for work. I would drink with my guys and come home drunk more often than not. I had my reasons to drink.

I shook my head. "Nah, the guys can have fun without me. No work to do either." I hadn't spent any time with Prima lately. It made me feel a bit guilty.

We made our way to the bedroom to get ready for bed. She went into our bathroom and started to remove her makeup.

"Do you love me, Prima?" My voice was calm. I didn't know why I'd asked her that after all these years.

"What?" She turned to me after she dried off her face.

"Do you love me?" I pressed.

Why would she? I barely saw the woman. She was like a stranger to me most days. We lived two different lives. We just happened to live under one roof.

"It's okay, you don't have to answer." I looked away, going back to changing.

Prima looked back at the mirror. "I-I don't know. Maybe?"

"Maybe? You either do or you don't." I chuckled.

"I don't want to talk about this right now Nico, I'm tired." She pushed past me, sitting on the bed.

"Come on, it's a simple question."

"Do you love me?" she questioned back.

"I- uh . . ."

"That's what I thought. Why did you ask, anyway?"

"The kids asked me." I admitted, sitting next to her.

She sat on the bed. "What did you say?"

"I said, 'of course I do.'" I definitely felt something for Prima. I didn't know what.

Prima blushed. "Goodnight, Nico," she replied softly, lying down.

"Goodnight, Prima."

CHAPTER TWENTY-FOUR

NICO

Prima wanted me to keep the kids occupied after school while she worked on getting things ready for the party the next day. Which usually meant Enzo was watching them.

I had work to get done. I half smiled as Enzo came in with Audrey and Coy, cones of ice cream in their hands. I had sent him to pick them up.

"Look what uncle Enzo got us!" Audrey screeched as she ran up to me, sitting on my lap. Some of her ice cream sprayed on my pants. "Sorry, Dad."

I chuckled. "That's alright, princess."

"Dad! Uncle Enzo took us to the park and there was an ice cream truck!" Coy was overcome with joy.

"I can tell." At least they were happy.

"Had to give them sugar before bringing them home," Enzo joked.

"Can you take them home? Prima should be done by now?"

"Sure." Enzo agreed before ushering the kids away. Audey gave me a sticky kiss on the cheek.

Sometimes I hated how much I ignored them. But they were kids. What did they know?

CHAPTER TWENTY-FIVE

PRIMA

We had rented the bowling alley for Coy's birthday party for a few hours. I had blown up blue and white balloons that matched the bowling alley, and we had matching plates, napkins, and cups. A chocolate cake that I had bought that morning was on the biggest table. The cake had 'Happy Birthday Coy' written in white frosting on top.

I was out of breath by the time I finished putting up the last balloon.

Pat and Enzo entered. Pat looked happy as ever with her baby bump. I wished I had what she had. They looked so in love. Enzo constantly talked about how happy he was to have a kid. Nico barely said a word when Audrey was born.

Coy and Audrey excitedly came up to Pat and Enzo, urging them to start bowling with them. Enzo joined them but Pat stayed behind.

"The party looks great!" Pat smiled.

"Thanks, it took some work." I chuckled.

Pat set a small box on the present table. "Where's Nico?"

"He's bringing the gifts from home. I forgot to grab them on the way out." I rubbed the back of my neck.

"Don't stress, Prima. It's going to be great." She placed a gentle hand on my shoulder.

Nico entered a moment later holding two presents, one from him and one from me. He had a grin on his face as he set them down. "Looks great," he told me as he kissed my cheek.

A few of Nico's friends started to scatter in as the party started. Nico left to talk to a few familiar faces.

Barb, Rosina, and Winnie arrived a little later. Rosina always seemed to be with Winnie. I assumed they were roommates.

The last people to arrive were Marie and her daughter, Mary. Mary hurried to go bowling with the kids.

"Hey, Prima!" Marie grinned as she walked over.

"This bitch," Nico mumbled under his breath.

Marie set her present down at the table. The table was now filled with presents. Nico's friends were clearly trying to show off.

Marie smiled widely. "So, Prima, quite the turn out, huh?"

"Yeah, thankfully," I replied. I felt Nico place a hand on my shoulder.

Marie smiled at Nico. "Little Coy is growing up to be a little man, isn't he? like his father."

"He is, just like his father."

Coy ran over to me. "Hey, Mom, can we cut the cake soon?"

"Do you want to open presents first?" I queried.

"Yeah, let's do that!" Coy squealed.

"Why don't you finish your game. Then we can, okay?" I told the boy.

"Okay!" Coy rushed off to finish bowling.

"Coy looks so much like you," Marie told me. "Not much like Nico though, huh?"

NICO

I had tuned out most of what Marie was saying. But that last comment snapped me back into the conversation. This bitch pissed me off.

"What's that supposed to mean?" I snapped.

"Just that he looks a lot like his mom, that's all," Marie defended.

"What, the bastard looks nothing like me, huh? Huh? Why the fuck do you always say 'huh?'" I wanted to strangle her.

I couldn't help myself. I'd kept the anger in for so long. Coy was not my son and never would be.

Prima placed a hand on my shoulder. People were starting to stare. "Nico, lets go bowling . . . "

"I just think he looks like Prima and not you. What's the problem with that?" Marie huffed. "You act like he's not your kid."

"Because he's not! Fuck off, Marie!" I shouted.

I looked at Prima. I went silent before storming out. I needed some air. I spat out one of the biggest secrets I was keeping. I didn't think it would have stayed a secret for long. The kid looked nothing like me.

Gianna Marie Ferraro

prima

I watched as everyone rushed to leave the party. It had just started, and now everyone was leaving. Everyone was murmuring and staring at me. My stomach twisted.

"Mom, what was dad talking about?" Coy's voice quivered.

"Why is Daddy so angry?" Audrey cried.

"Nothing, honey, he meant nothing. "I knelt down to their level, pulling them into a hug.

"He said he wasn't my dad. What did he mean?" I could feel Coy's heart pounding.

"He meant . . . nothing." I couldn't look at him.

"Mom, who's my dad?" I watched as tears started to stream down the little boy's cheeks.

"Audrey, go outside with your father. Okay?" I told Audrey once the room was empty.

I watched as Audrey hesitated but went outside.

"Mom, answer my question!" Coy cried, "I'm not stupid."

My face fell. He needed to know. I wished he wasn't so young. I took a deep breath. "He was a bad man, okay? But Nico, he cares about you. You're his son even if it's not by blood."

"Who's my dad?" He sniffled.

"His name was Ray Gallo. You're too young to know the story, okay? I'll tell you when you're older, but for now, I need you to trust me. He was a bad man, and your father is . . . a good man. Let's pack up your presents and cake and go home, okay?"

"I hate him," Coy snapped.

"Who do you hate?"

"My dad. Nico, whatever you want to call him!" Coy shouted, "I hate him for lying to me!"

"Don't say that." I wanted to cry. "Please don't say that."

He crossed his arms over his chest. "Why? He hates me."

"He doesn't hate you, honey." I softly placed a hand on his cheek.

"I don't believe you," he cried as he pulled away. "He lied to me."

I didn't know what to say for a moment. "Adults lie. It's hard, but they do."

He looked up at me. "You lied to me too . . . "

My stomach dropped as I asked, "Do you hate me?"

"No." He sniffled.

"Then why should you hate him?"

"Because he's not my dad."

I let out a heavy sigh. "Let's go home, okay?" I felt defeated.

NICO

I let out a heavy sigh as I lit my cigarette. Everyone walked past me as they left the party—they wouldn't dare stare at me.

I almost fell over when I felt someone grab my leg. I looked down to see my little Audrey. Her big brown eyes were filled with tears as she stared up at me.

"Daddy, why are you so angry?" she asked through her sniffles.

"I'm not mad at you, princess," I told her with a heavy sigh, patting her head. "So don't worry about it."

"Dad?" Her little voice squeaked.

"Yeah?" I took a puff of my cigarette.

"Do you love us?" Audrey questioned.

She was so innocent, so pure. I let out a breath as I peeled the small child off my leg. I put my cigarette out before getting to her level.

"Yes, I love you and your mom very much."

"What about Coy?" Audrey tilted her head.

I gave her a fake smile. "Him too," I lied.

We took the kids, along with the cake and the presents, to spend the weekend with Vinnie. Once we were home, I immediately went to the fridge to grab a beer.

"I'm going out soon," I told Prima before chugging half a beer.

"Nico. Why did you do that?" She gripped her skirt.

"He's old enough to know the truth. Everyone probably knew I wasn't the father, anyway. At least they know you didn't cheat this time." I finished the other half of the beer.

She let go of her skirt. "Nico, he's your son."

I glared at her before throwing my beer bottle, missing her head by an inch, shattering it on the wall. "He's not my fucking son!"

I had hated that kid since he was born. The more he grew, the more I despised him. He wasn't a baby anymore. I had to hold myself back from punching him in the face every time I looked at him.

Prima started to sob. I watched as she slid down the wall. She started shaking as I got closer to her.

I groaned. "What did you want me to do? Get rid of him? No, I couldn't. You couldn't. I've kept it up for so long. The older he gets, the more he looks like Ray. The more he looks like that fucking monster. He's just a replacement for Frank."

I watched as she cried. She started to pick up the broken pieces of the beer bottle. "You wanted to know if I loved you, Nico? I don't. I can't after this."

My face dropped. I was going to say something. But what would I even say? Instead, I left her there crying on the floor.

Gianna Marie Ferraro

prima

I woke up to Nico picking me up off the floor. I must've fallen asleep there. Nico sat on the couch, holding me close to his chest. I could smell alcohol on his breath and a perfume I didn't recognize. I didn't say anything.

"I'm sorry, Prima." Nico whispered. "I'm sorry. I love you, Prima, more than anything."

"I love you too," I mumbled. *Did I mean it?*

He was quiet for a moment. "I don't mean to hurt you."

"I know, Nico," I told him as he sat me on the bed.

He laid his head on my shoulder, letting out a deep breath. I wrapped my arms around him as we both sat there in silence.

CHAPTER TWENTY-SIX

prima

My father poured me a cup of coffee before sitting across from me at the table.

"You doing okay, Prima?" he questioned as he stirred his coffee.

"Did the kids have fun?" I asked him.

"Yeah, they did. They played outside a lot." He smiled. "Like you and your sisters used to do."

"Yeah." I sipped my coffee. "That was a long time ago."

I missed those days, when we would go outside and skin our knees without a care in the world. That stopped after their divorce.

"So . . . he's Ray's kid?" he questioned bluntly.

"Yeah," I breathed.

"I thought so." My father puffed. "Everyone did, actually."

"Nico was so angry after the party." I could feel tears swell up. "I don't know why he snapped."

"The guys at the bar kept giving him shit," my father admitted. "I'm not going to deny I was one of them. They kept bringing up Ray . . . and Sill."

Sill. I hadn't heard his name out loud in a while. It stung.

"Did Coy say anything to you . . . or Audrey?"

"Audrey seemed more confused than anything. Coy was upset. Whenever Audrey wasn't around, he kept asking me if I knew Ray."

My mind was racing, but all I said was, "I'm glad he at least waited until she wasn't around. Did you tell him?"

"Not much. I said he was a bad man that did bad things to his mother." He sipped his coffee.

I took a sip of mine. "I don't know how I can fix this."

"You can't." He looked me in the eye. "Nico ruined any chance of that. But the kid needed to know the truth sooner or later."

He was right, there was nothing I could do except hope that Coy would get over it and Nico would continue treating him as his son. The most I could do was hope.

"Why did you want me to come over?" I questioned bluntly, changing the subject.

He brought his gaze back to the coffee. "I wanted to see you, that's all."

I watched him light a cigarette. "I know I haven't been around. I know I should try to at least talk to you. You are the only daughter near me." He took a puff from his cigarette. "It's not like your sisters call or write. I mean, Silvia can't . . . You're right under my nose and I never even try to talk to you. You never try to talk to me either. I guess that is why your mom gave you that nickname. Silent Prima Donna." He let out a small chuckle. "I'm not a good father. I wasn't meant to be one. But I guess being with my grandkids helped me see I could've tried harder."

I took his free hand slowly and gave him a reassuring smile. I didn't know what to say. He left our family when I was young. I barely knew anything about him.

"It's never too late to try." My voice was soft.

He gave me a smile. "I'm glad to hear that." He took another puff of his cigarette, blowing the smoke into the air before letting go of my hand. "Things okay with Nico?"

"They're fine." I took a sip of my coffee.

"He's a good man. He doesn't hit you, right?"

"No . . . but father we've been married almost twelve years, and you ask this now?"

"Just making sure. I don't want to be known as a worse father for setting up my kid with a guy who hits his wife."

"Coy said he hates Nico." I kept my voice quiet. The kids were playing in the other room.

"Do you blame him? The kid found out he's not his father. He'll get over it."

"Will he?"

"You don't hate me, that I know of, and I walked out on you girls."

"I don't . . . I never have."

Why would I hate him? He was doing what was best for us. It was better than hearing them argue all the time. I wished he'd been in my life more while I was growing up.

"See, if you can get over it, he can too. At least Nico is in his life."

"Mamma was in my life . . . " I turned away, facing the wall.

"Well, your mom was a crazy bitch. I don't know why I married that woman. I was too fucking drunk all the time. When I sobered up, I realized how much of a cunt she is. Now I'm back to being drunk."

"Dad, the kids are in the other room." I cleared my throat as Audrey rushed by him and pulled me into a hug.

"Mamma! Can we go home?" She screeched.

"Soon. We can head out in a few minutes, okay?" I ruffled her hair.

"I want to see Daddy," Audrey whined. "I miss him."

"Your father won't be home when we get home, okay?" I tried to smile.

"Where is he?" She looked at me, confused.

"He went to work," I told her.

"Coy said that Dad isn't his dad. Is Nico my dad?" She'd asked the dreaded question.

"Yes, Nico is your dad." I placed a hand on her cheek. "You have his eyes."

"Is Coy—"

"Why don't you go get your things?" I cut her off. "Coy! Time to go"

I knew Audrey would eventually figure things out.. I wasn't ready to say that her brother was actually her half-brother, not out loud.

PART FIVE

Prima, Nico, Audrey and Coy

1978

Gianna Marie Ferraro

CHAPTER TWENTY-SEVEN

PRIMA

I could hear the school bell ring from the park bench. I let out a deep sigh as I looked up at the clouds. The sky was filled with them, the sun barely peeking out. Audrey was coming with me to get our hair done after school.

I smiled as I saw my little girl, who was now almost sixteen, approaching. She was wearing a sleeveless pink dress that hit mid-thigh with a white turtleneck underneath.

I stood up from the bench and went to greet her.

"How was your day, Audrey?"

"Fine," she huffed. "I got Coy's schoolwork."

I shook my head in disappointment. "Did he skip again?"

"Of course he did. What else does he do these days?" She moved her blonde hair behind her ear.

It scared me how much she was starting to look like me. It was like me and Mamma. I didn't want her to end up like me.

"Your father isn't going to be happy about this." I started to walk with her.

"Don't tell Dad. You know how it is. They always end up in a screaming match." Audrey huffed.

She was right. It felt like every time Coy and Nico were in the same room, they got into a fight. One time Coy even punched Nico. I didn't even know what half their fights were about.

"You look tired, Mom. Did you sleep?" Audrey questioned.

I nodded. I hadn't been sleeping much the past few days. The stress of Coy constantly skipping school and Nico's drinking made me restless.

What had Coy gotten himself into? I hadn't met any of his friends, but from what Audrey had told me, none of them went to school regularly.

We made it to the salon and were greeted by a small child grabbing my legs. The salon was the one thing that had barely changed. Pat and Enzo's daughter, Frankie, was there often and was now grabbing my legs.

"Prima!" she screeched.

"Frankie, calm the fuck down." Barb rolled her eyes.

"Hey! Don't swear around my kid, asshole." Pat groaned.

"Hi, Frankie." I chuckled, picking her up. "How was school?"

"Fine, my teacher was mean though. She made me go on timeout." She huffed.

"Well, if you didn't make that kid lick a frog, you wouldn't have been put in time out." Pat snickered. "Little demon child."

Frankie was an adorable child. She had red curly hair, like Pat's, with brown eyes like Enzo's. She was shorter than most of the kids her age, which made her look younger.

I set the child down before settling onto the salon chair next to Audrey.

"How's school been?" Pat questioned Audrey.

"Fine, I've been looking at collages," Audrey told her as she flipped through a magazine.

"That's great, anywhere you want to go?"

"Duke or Brown, maybe. Somewhere decent would be nice."

"Oh, so you're smart?" Pat chuckled. "You got this, kid."

"Thanks, Aunt Pat." She smiled.

I hadn't talked to Nico about Audrey's future. I was too scared. I didn't want her to end up in an arranged marriage like me. I wanted her to go to college. That's all she wanted. I didn't know if Nico would agree with it.

"You want the same thing as always, Prima?" Pat questioned, playing with my hair.

"Yeah."

"Mom, you get the same hair every time. It went out of style ten years ago. Get something new," Audrey insisted.

"But your father likes it this way," I replied softly.

"He can get used to a new way." Audrey handed me her magazine.

I flipped through the magazine for a moment before I ran into a picture of Farrah Fawcett. I did like her hair, but I wasn't sure Nico would.

"That one?" Pat questioned. "You would look good in that one."

Gianna Marie Ferraro

coy

I slicked my hair back into a ponytail and balanced a cigarette on my lips as I watched Enzo's car drive by. He drove by the park every Thursday at one in the afternoon, probably making his rounds for Nico.

Enzo was like an uncle to me. Mom never talked about her sisters, and I wasn't even sure whether Nico had siblings. Enzo was like family to us.

I knew Enzo moved Nico's money once a week. I loved Enzo, but Nico didn't deserve what he had.

I made this plan up with my friend Ricky a few weeks ago. We studied Enzo every Thursday. All we had to do was wait in a small pavilion out of sight, wait until Enzo stops at the restaurant, follow him into the alley, then knock him out and take the money. It was foolproof.

"When does he stop?" My friend Ricky tapped his foot impatiently.

"Soon." I took the cigarette between my fingers, blowing smoke before I threw it to the ground.

We both watched as Uncle Enzo's car passed by and parked next to the alleyway.

There was a heavy-set man with Enzo, the man was in a brown suit. His hair was black and slicked back.

I had never seen him before, not even around the neighborhood.

"Is there normally someone with him?" Rick looked at me, puzzled.

"No, there's not." I groaned. "We can try again next week.

"Come on, dude! You promised me cash. We're going to get it." Ricky pulled his pistol out openly.

I took it from him quickly, shoving it in my pants. "Do you want to get pinched?! It's the middle of the fucking day. Anyone could see."

We watched Enzo and the mystery man get out of the car. The mystery man was carrying a duffle bag. This was our shot. I put a black ski mask on and signaled Ricky to move. We followed the two men down an alleyway slowly. Apparently not slow enough.

I grabbed Enzo's shoulder, about to pistol whip him in the head, when I was punched in the side of the face. It sent me flying into the alley wall.

I could feel blood start to drip from my mouth as the mystery man punched me in the face once more before Enzo stopped him. "Hey, quit it, that's Nico's kid."

Enzo pulled my mask off. I could see Ricky run out of the corner of my eye. *Pussy.*

I didn't know how Enzo recognized me with the mask on. It could've been my hair, but lots of guys had long hair these days.

"What the hell do you think you're doing?" Enzo calmly asked.

"Don't worry about it." I spit blood on the ground.

"Go home, kid. My friend here could've done a lot worse. You're lucky." Enzo shook his head in disappointment.

"Lucky? How am I lucky?"

"That you have a powerful father. If you were anyone else's kid, I would've punched you myself." Enzo told me as he helped me off the ground.

"He's not my dad." I shot him a glare.

"Go home, Coy," Enzo demanded.

I dragged myself home, wondering what I was going to tell mom. My face throbbed. I was pretty sure I'd broken a few teeth.

If Nico found out I had tried to rob him, I'd be screwed. If Mom found out, she'd scold me and try to ground me.

Why did Enzo have someone with him? He never had anyone with him. This was my one chance to actually make some cash and get out of this shit hole.

Gianna Marie Ferraro

NICO

It was an oddly quiet day when Mike came back. I used to talk to Mike all the time. After Zeno died, he left the neighborhood and went to make a name for himself in Philadelphia. But now he was back.

Mike looked old. His hair was all gray, and there was a bald spot on the back of his head. His eyes drooped, but they were the same shade of blue.

"It's good to see you, Nico." He pulled me into a hug.

"It's good to see you too." I smiled, pulling away. We both sat down at a table. I handed the man a cigar.

"Thank you," he told me as he took a seat.

"What brings you back here?" I questioned him.

"My mother died," he told me as he shoved the cigar in his pocket. "The woman was almost one hundred."

"I'm sorry for your loss." I placed a hand on his shoulder.

"She was old as shit." He chuckled. "So, I heard you have kids now."

"Yeah, a daughter. Audrey," I told him.

"I thought you had a son too."

"No, just a daughter."

He didn't need to know about Coy.

"My son saw your daughter with you the other day. Said she's pretty." Mike smiled. "He wanted to marry her." He laughed.

"Maybe we could arrange something." I leaned in.

I knew Audrey wanted to go to college. That's not what I wanted for her. She would be a good stay-at-home wife like her mom. That's what I expected.

"Let's set something up this Friday," Mike proposed.

"Sounds good to me."

I didn't even think about asking Prima. She'd had an arranged marriage, and I was the man of the house. Why would she care? She never stood up to me unless it involved Coy, but he was the problem child, not Audrey.

Gianna Marie Ferraro

AUDREY

Mom stepped out to take Frankie to the park. While I was getting my hair done. Pat hummed softly as she cut my hair.

"So, doll, seeing anyone?" Pat chuckled.

"W-what? No." I blushed.

That was a lie. I was seeing someone. He wasn't from the neighborhood though. We went to school together. We were in the same English class. His name was Andrés.

He was the sweetest guy, handsome too. Most of the girls in school fawned over him. He had the looks and the smarts. What more could you want?

I didn't tell anyone because he was, to say it bluntly, Puerto Rican. I knew my dad wouldn't want to see me with anyone who wasn't Italian. He was the only one I was really worried about.

The only person who knew we were dating was my friend Mary, and that was because we were best friends. She was the only one who didn't ditch me after Coy's birthday.

"Whatever you say," Pat replied as she snipped a piece of my hair.

I hesitated before speaking. "Aunt Pat?"

"Yeah, doll?"

"Can I tell you something?"

"Whatever is said in the salon, stays in the salon."

My stomach twisted but I knew I could trust her.

I bit my lip. "I may be seeing someone."

She practically squealed, "What's the lucky guy's name?"

"That, I won't say . . . " I kept my voice low.

"Oh? So, what's wrong with him?" She lowered her voice.

I came to Pat with most of the problems I couldn't go to Mom with. She was easier to talk to about certain things. Mom was quiet and kept to herself most of the time, unlike Pat.

"He's not Italian," I replied softly.

She waved her scissors around as she said, "I see . . . You don't think your dad will like that, huh?"

"Not one bit." I let out a breath. "But he's an amazing guy. He reminds me of Uncle Enzo."

"Well, I don't see a problem then." She let out a soft chuckle. "Maybe bring it up to your mom. She won't mind."

We both went silent as Mom entered. She took a seat on the chair next to me.

Gianna Marie Ferraro

PRIMA

After what felt like forever, I walked out of the salon feeling like a new woman with my hair. A part of me was still scared of what Nico would think. Audrey also got her hair cut into a soft bob. It looked great with her soft curls.

We stopped at the bar to see Nico who was currently working. He wanted us to come by to see what we'd had done. He was in the back room like he always was. It was only him and my father.

Both men turned to us, Nico looking me up and down. "Don't you two ladies look nice."

"Do you like Mom's new hair?" Audrey pressed.

"Yeah, I do, it looks good." He gave us a smile.

I couldn't tell if he was being genuine or not. I guessed I would find out later.

Gianna Marie Ferraro

NICO

"Have you seen Coy?" Prima hesitantly asked.

"I saw him running around with his jerk-off friends a few hours ago," Vinnie told us.

"Let him ruin his life."

Prima stayed silent for a moment before saying, "We'll see you at home . . . "

"Audrey, why don't you go home? I want to spend some time with my wife."

Audrey nodded.

"I'll walk you home, sweetheart" Vinnie stood up with a smile.

We watched Audrey and Vinnie leave the room. I grabbed Prima's hand and pulled her onto my lap. "I do really like the new hair," I told her, "but, why would you let Audrey cut hers so short?"

Prima shifted slightly. "She wanted it and it's the new style."

" I wanted to talk to you about something." I averted my gaze. "I have a friend who is interested in Audrey."

"Interested how?" Prima's voice shook.

"He wants to take her on a few dates. Well, his son does," I told her.

She let out a sigh of relief. I didn't think she wanted Audrey to marry an old man like me.

"I'll talk to her."

"No, you'll tell her she's going on a date tomorrow night. Got it?" I stated firmly.

She nodded, keeping silent for a moment before saying, "Nico, can we talk about Audrey's future?"

"I have it planned out already," I told her. "Go home, Prima."

Her voice shook but she remained calm. "Let her go to college, Nico."

"I'll think about it," I lied.

"Nico, please give me this one thing." She could see right through me. "I never got to go. She's almost a grown woman now."

"Prima, I'm done talking about this." I glared at her. "Go home."

Prima turned quickly. I watched her leave as Enzo came in.

"How'd it go, Enzo?" I queried.

Enzo took a deep breath. "Well, your son. He's an idiot."

"Yeah, so? What happened?" I groaned.

He messed with this shirt collar. "He tried to rob us with a little buddy of his. We stopped him though, don't worry."

"He tried to do what?"

He cleared his throat, seemingly regretting telling me. "He came at me with a gun and tried to take the money. Don't worry, Leo got him good." Enzo sat in the chair across from me.

What did that bastard think? He was going to rob me? Was he insane? He was a boy trying to mess with a man.

Gianna Marie Ferraro

Grandpa was quiet for most of the walk home. We were almost a block away when he finally said, "You remind me of my daughter Silvia."

The comment was random. Grandpa never talked about Mom's sisters.

"Why do you say that?" I questioned hesitantly.

"Silvia was quiet and reserved but still had so much spirit." He looked ahead of us longingly.

What did he mean by *was*? I didn't want to push. I was lucky to even hear her name.

"Don't tell your mother," he started. "I want to tell you a secret."

It was odd Grandpa wanted to tell me anything. We rarely talked anymore. *He wanted to tell me a secret?*

"Silvia was sentenced to the electric chair. I just found out she's been dead for years." His chuckle was hollow as tears pricked his eyes.

My face paled. How the hell was I supposed to keep a secret like that? My aunt was sentenced to death? I'd heard she was in jail but that was it.

"I'm sorry, I needed to tell someone." He turned his attention to his feet.

I grabbed his hand gently and let out a heavy sigh. "Don't worry, Grandpa."

I felt like I was going to throw up. I tried to stay as composed as possible.

We were quiet the rest of the way home. I wanted to go into the bedroom and cry, but I heard a groan from the couch. I walked over to it calmly, until I was standing over Coy who was lying there. His face was bloody and bruised.

"What the hell happened to you?"

"Nothing." Coy huffed." What happened to you?"

I ignored the tears that wanted to pour out, trying to stop them from falling. I wiped my eyes quickly before turning my attention back to Coy.

"Doesn't look like nothing."

"I messed around with Gerogio's girl, that's all," he told me as he sat up.

"You idiot, Gerogio already hates you." I crossed my arms.

prima

I went home alone. Once there, I caught Audrey scolding Coy who was sitting on the couch.

"Why do you still hang out with those fuck heads?" Audrey hadn't seen me come in. "When they do shit like this to you?"

"Don't even start, Audrey," Coy snapped, standing up. "At least I have friends."

I noticed he had a huge bruise on the side of his face and his eye looked swollen.

"What happened?" I finally spoke up. I kept my tone leveled.

"Nothing, Ma." Coy grumbled. "Just got into a disagreement, that's all."

"Your face is all black and blue," I replied. I hurried to the kitchen to get some ice out of the icebox.

"Well, maybe if you didn't skip school to fuck Georgio's girl." I could almost hear Audrey roll her eyes.

I returned to the living room, handing Coy the bag of ice. "Your father isn't going to be happy about this . . . "

"He's not my dad!" Coy shouted, I flinched, and he paused for a moment before sighing. "Sorry, Mom, I didn't mean to yell."

Coy had put on a 'tough guy' facade for the past few years, but on the inside, I knew he was still my sweet little boy. His hair was longer, and he mainly kept it in a ponytail. He usually wore a leather jacket and a plain T-shirt. He was definitely handsome, but he looked so much like Ray, sometimes it was scary.

I watched as Coy stormed out of the room, a bag of ice on his face.

I turned to face Audrey. "Your father wanted me to talk to you."

"About what?" She looked at me, puzzled.

"He has a date for you on Friday . . ."

She wrinkled her nose. "It's not an old man, is it?"

I shook my head. "Apparently someone around your age."

"But Mom . . . " She bit her lip.

"I can't say no to your father. Neither can you. You know that."

"What? Does he want me to marry this kid?"

"I don't know." I averted my gaze. "He told me you two had to go out on Friday, and that was it."

My stomach churned. I hated making her go. I could try talking to Nico, but I doubted it would do much.

"Mom, I'll be fine." She gave me a reassuring smile as she placed her hand on my shoulder.

I frowned slightly. "Are you sure?"

"Maybe it won't be so bad?"

I heard the front door open, and we both turned to see Coy going to leave.

"Where are you going?" Audrey crossed her arms.

"Out." Coy stuck his hands in his pockets.

"I'm going to start making dinner. Will you be back?" I didn't know how to stop him.

"I'm not hungry. Don't wait up," Coy replied before starting to leave. Nico blocked his exit.

"Your mother wants you to stay for dinner." Nico narrowed his eyes. "You're staying and we need to talk."

"About what, old man?" Coy crossed his arms.

"I heard the shit you pulled today." Nico grabbed his shirt collar.

"Nico, don't—" I went quiet as he glared at me.

Although they were almost the same height, Nico was still much larger than Coy. Coy worked out, but he was still rather skinny.

"I did what I had to do." Coy pulled himself away.

"Yeah? You had to steal from one of my guys? If you want to work for me someday, you gotta show me some respect, boy."

"Why would I want to work for you?" Coy started to walk down the hall.

"Where are you going?" Nico groaned.

"My room," Coy replied, slamming the door.

"Audrey, go start dinner," Nico demanded.

"The chicken's in the fridge," I told her as she quietly left the room.

"Do you want to know what your son did today?" Nico crossed his arms. "He stole from Enzo, well tried to. That's why he has a fucking black eye."

"Enzo punched him?" I raised a brow.

"No, but his partner did. That kid needs to get his life in check."

"He told me a friend punched him."

"With his friends, it's believable. But no, not this time." Nico placed his hands on my waist. "I'm going to take him out tonight."

"He has school in the morning." I had a gut feeling I needed Coy to stay home.

"Like he goes?" Nico scoffed. "I'm taking him out, and that's that."

"Okay. I'm going to go help Audrey with dinner."

I wanted to protect Coy, but how? If I disobeyed Nico, who knew what he would do? But if I didn't protect my son, I would be a bad mother.

Gianna Marie Ferraro

coy

I was silent the whole ride to the bar. I could sense Nico's fury. He mumbled to himself quietly enough that I couldn't hear.

The car jerked as we parked. I shot him a glare before getting out. He grabbed my shoulder once out of the car, forcing me toward the bar door. Something told me I should run. I couldn't. *Would he kill me?* Mom would never forgive him if he did.

It seemed like the bar could tell Nico was angry. Everyone quieted down as we entered. He took me to the back room. It had been so long since I had been back there. Probably since I was a kid.

Enzo was back there, with Grandpa and a few other guys, including the man in the brown suit who punched me earlier.

Nico patted my back, hard. "Say hi, Coy."

I glared at Nico. "Hello," I grumbled.

"Why the long face?" the punchy one questioned.

"Looks like you did a number on him, Leo." Nico chuckled.

"Well, he was trying to steal from his pops. I had to." Leo hummed.

"He's not my dad," I breathed.

"And you'll never be my son." I watched Nico clench his fists.

Nico's fist landed on my stomach, causing the air to go out of me. Was this why Nico brought me here? To beat the shit out of me away from mom?

Before I could do anything, I felt Leo restrain my arms from behind. I wrestled to break free from Leo's grasp. I watched Enzo sip his drink. Another punch to the stomach.

"Uncle Enzo! Please," I begged. "Stop him!"

Enzo looked away. His face looked stern, but his eyes were screaming.

"You need to be taught a lesson!" Nico spat on me. "Think you're tough? You can steal from me? Just because I'm married to your mom doesn't mean I'm going to go easy on you. You're still Ray's son."

Ray. Nico always brought up Ray. I didn't know anything about the guy. Mom never talked about him since telling me his name. Nico hated his guts.

I watched Enzo get up from his chair as I was pushed to the ground. A kick landed on my chest. Nico held his foot there. I could barely move.

Enzo left the room, ignoring my pleas. Why would he help me? He was one of Nico's clowns in this fucked up circus.

I fought as hard as I could to stand. It felt like more guys had started showing up, all of them kicking me while I writhed on the floor.

AUDREY

I helped mom with the dishes after Coy and Dad left for the bar. We were both silent, listening to the water run in the sink. She scrubbed and I dried. I had never noticed before, but she had faint scars on both her wrists.

"Mom . . . " I had to tell her. "Can I talk to you about something?"

"What is it, honey?" She kept her eyes on the soapy water.

"Do you know what happened to your sisters?" I felt like that was a good way to start. Maybe she knew?

She let out a deep sigh. "Stella went to take care of your cousin, and Silvia . . . " She went quiet. "She's in jail. Why the sudden interest in my sisters?"

"Grandpa told me that—" I cleared my throat. "Never mind." I didn't know how I was going to tell her. *I shouldn't have been the one doing this.*

Mom gave me a small smile. *Maybe she already knew?* Maybe she saw it on the news or in the paper. It's not every day someone gets the electric chair.

Gianna Marie Ferraro

NICO

I left Coy passed out cold in the corner on the floor. He got what he deserved. *Would Prima be happy?* No. but the kid needed to be taught a lesson. She couldn't do shit.

"You're too hard on him." Enzo finally spoke up. "He's just a dumb kid."

"He needed to be taught a lesson." I placed a cigarette on my lips and lit it. "It's none of your business, Enzo."

"I didn't mean to overstep," Enzo started. "But you did raise the kid."

"What, like this is my fault?!" I shouted. I could hear Coy groan.

"No, no, that's not what I'm saying." Enzo shook his head.

"Don't you have to get home for dinner?" I glared at him.

I didn't know where Enzo was going with that, but this was none of his goddamn business.

Enzo left as I watched some of the guys put out their cigarettes on Coy's arms. I didn't care. I wasn't going to stop them.

Gianna Marie Ferraro

coy

I woke up a few hours later, still on the floor. There was a pillow under my head, at least. I could smell cigarettes. The air was foggy above me.

"Good, you're awake." Nico was sitting, smoking with Leo and a few other guys. Enzo was gone. "Go to the bathroom and clean yourself up. Once that's done, we'll go."

It took a couple of minutes, but I finally found the strength to stand. I made my way, painfully, to the bathroom. Everything burned.

I took my jacket off carefully and looked in the mirror. He hadn't touched my face or neck, only the places that could be hidden by clothing.

My arms were covered in fresh bruises and blood. I noticed a few scattered burns from cigarettes. The asshole put his cigarette out on me.

I cleaned the blood off, cleaned my hair, then left the bathroom. I walked like nothing had happened even though my body wanted to collapse.

Gianna Marie Ferraro

pRIMA

I couldn't sleep. Audrey had gone to bed a long time ago, but I stayed awake. Nico never wanted to spend time with Coy. What was he doing?

The door swung open around one in the morning. Coy looked even more pissed off than before. He marched to his room without a word. I noticed he limped slightly.

Nico sat down next to me on the couch. "What are you doing up?" His knuckles were red.

"I couldn't sleep. I was waiting for you," I replied. *Something was wrong.*

"Go get some rest." Nico smiled, then kissed my cheek.

I looked at my feet. "Nico, what happened?"

"Nothing. Go to bed," he replied firmly.

Nico got up and went to the fridge to grab a beer. I reluctantly headed to the bedroom. As I walked down the hall, I could hear a faint sob coming from Coy's room. I hesitated but knocked.

It took a moment but Coy cracked open the door.

"Yeah, Ma?" I could hear him sniffle.

"Do you need to talk?" I questioned softly.

Coy left the door open and made his way to his bed and sat down, giving me the okay to enter. I shut the door behind me.

"What did he do?" I sat next to him, wiping a tear from his cheek.

Coy didn't cry that often. That's what worried me the most.

Coy wiped his eyes. "Don't worry, I'm fine." I grabbed his hand carefully, noticing a mark. It looked like a cigarette burn. It was fresh. The sleeve of his jacket moved slightly, revealing a bruise on his arm.

"Take off the jacket"

"Mom," Coy protested.

"Take it off." My voice was firm.

He hesitantly removed his jacket, groaning in pain as he did so. His arms were covered in bruises.

I stood up without another word, then marched to the living room. I could hear Coy call for me, but I ignored him.

"Nico, what the fuck did you do?" I could feel my face getting warm. I was rarely angry, but he'd hurt my son. I couldn't forgive that.

"I taught him a lesson. Why are you so mad? I didn't kill him." He stood up and took a swig of his beer.

"You don't fucking touch my kid!" I shouted. "What the hell is wrong with you?!"

"Calm down, he got what he deserved."

I didn't know what came over me, but before I knew it, I slapped him. I hit him right across the face. I could see the look of shock on Nico's face before it turned to vexation. He grabbed my wrists tightly.

"You think you can fucking hit me?! You fucking whore! I've never laid my hands on you, and you fucking hit me?!"

Gianna Marie Ferraro

coy

I got off my bed as fast as I could, basically limping to the living room.

"Nico, I'm sorry. You're hurting me!" Mom whimpered.

I could hear Audrey's door open. "Mom, what's going on?" she sleepily asked.

"Go back to your room, sweetie." Mom's voice shook.

"Dad, what the hell?" I joined in.

"Both of you, this is between me and your mother!" Nico shouted before dragging Mom toward the bedroom.

Audrey hurried to my side. We watched Nico push her into the room before slamming the door. I could hear a thud.

"You hurt our son! How could you do that?!" I heard her yell.

"Coy, what do we do?" Audrey was almost in tears.

The two of us hurried to the door and tried to open it. It was locked, of course.

"He's not my son!" Nico was enraged.

"You're as bad as Ray."

We heard another thud. I pushed my shoulder into the door. No matter how much it hurt, I had to try to help.

Nico stormed out of the room before I could push into it again. He walked straight past us and out the front door. Audrey was the first to rush to Mom's side. She was sitting on the floor, tears streaming down her cheeks. There was a hole in the wall, next to where her head would've been if she was standing.

CHAPTER TWENTY-EIGHT

AUDREY

I ended up staring at my ceiling until my alarm went off. *What even happened last night?* It was like a fever dream. I sighed as I got out of bed, the smell of food coming from the kitchen

Coy's bedroom door was still closed as I made my way to the kitchen.

Mom's hands were shaking as she made breakfast.

"Mom, are you okay? Is dad home?" I questioned her.

"I'm fine, and no." She didn't look fine.

I watched her flip the pancakes before I spoke. "Mom, did he hurt you?"

"I'm okay." She smiled at me. "Why don't you stay home today?"

"Can't," I told her. "I have a test I can't miss."

"Okay." She stared at the counter as she plated the pancake.

Why did she always act like she was okay? She rarely fought with Dad, but this might have been the worst fight I'd ever seen them have.

I tapped my pencil on the corner of my test paper. I couldn't stop thinking about the night before. I couldn't help but question *why?*

"Pencils down," the teacher demanded, breaking me out of my spell.

"Shit," I mumbled to myself. I had only filled in half the questions.

I let out a soft sigh before glancing around, making eye contact with Andrés. He had a strand of his shaggy brown hair covering one of his eyes as he gave me a shy smile.

We met each other in the hallway after class. He grabbed my hand. I pulled away.

"Not in public, Dre," I mumbled.

"Come one, why not? It's hand holding. It's not like one of your Dad's friends goes to our school." Andrés chuckled softly.

"I know, but if Coy sees . . . "

"Coy, who never goes to school?" He chuckled.

He was right. Coy was never in school, so what was there to hide? If he did see us, would he even say anything? It wasn't like he cared about me that much.

I grabbed his hand and started to walk down the hall with him to lunch. My heart was pounding. This was the most physical contact we'd made in public.

I was afraid everyone would be staring at us and whispering, but no one seemed to care as we walked down the halls.

I watched a locker close. I knew that locker. It was Coy's. *What the hell was he doing at school?* His face had a bruise on it, but the rest of his wounds were covered up.

I watched him as he looked us up and down before turning to walk away. I let go of Andrés' hand. "I'll meet you at lunch."

I followed Coy down an empty hallway. He stopped once we got to the end. "Are you crazy?"

"Why are you here, Coy? You never come to school." I huffed.

"I didn't want to miss my finals. But that doesn't matter. Why were you holding hands with that guy?"

I hesitated. "He's my boyfriend."

"Nico will kill you if he finds out, you know that?" he groaned. "Stupid."

"Dad wouldn't do that." I looked away from him.

"Well, he'd kill him then." Coy snapped. "Be careful, Audrey. "

"Since when do you care what I do? You've barely talked to me since we were kids, and we live in the same house," I snapped.

Coy frowned. "I do care about you."

"You're my big brother," I replied firmly. "You never act like it."

"I just want you to be careful, okay? If he finds out . . ."

"I know that, Coy. but he won't find out. It's not like he has someone watching us all the time."

"How do you know? He has someone tailing Mom all the time," he pointed out.

He was right. We didn't know if Dad had someone watching us at school. Even though none of us said it out loud, we would always feel someone watching us when we were with Mom.

"I'll be more careful. I'm sorry"

"Don't apologize, Audrey."

"You need to be more careful too. Dad did a number on you last night."

Gianna Marie Ferraro

coy

"Yeah, I know." I ran a hand through my hair.

"I'll see you at home." She let out a sigh. "Be careful."

"You too."

Nico wasn't a man to be messed with. I'd definitely seen more than I should have in my childhood, even before I had started to hate him.

He would take me to the bar every Saturday. I used to think he wanted me to get into his business with him when I got older. I would watch him beat up other men, kiss women that weren't my mom, and scream orders. I never told anyone what I'd seen. I watched quietly. Audrey didn't know, and I wanted to keep it that way.

I wanted to start my own gang one day. I already had a decent group of guys set up. We needed a plan. We needed to think smarter than Nico. I needed to take him down

I snapped out of my thoughts as Audrey walked away. I let out a deep sigh before deciding I would skip the rest of my classes. Fuck finals. There was no way I could graduate at this point anyway. I was surprised I hadn't gotten kicked out yet.

Gianna Marie Ferraro

PRIMA

The bubbles from my bath covered most of my body. I sank into the water when I heard Nico come in. It was around 11:00 a.m. I could hear him groan as he entered the bedroom, probably at seeing the hole he had put in the wall.

There was a gentle knock on the door. "Baby, you in there?"

"Yeah." I dunked my head under the water. When I came up, Nico was in the bathroom.

"I'm sorry I pushed you last night." He sat next to the bathtub.

"Are you going to apologize for beating up Coy?" I snapped.

"No."

"Then I won't forgive you." I watched the bubbles pop.

"Come on, Prima. The brat deserved it. He tried to steal from me!"

"Can you leave me alone? Please."

"No. I can't leave you alone until you forgive me."

"Nico, how can I? You deal with everything with violence." I turned from him like a child, spilling some water from the tub. "I thought you would be different with my child."

Nico stood up. "Dinner. Tonight. We are going out, so look pretty. Got it?"

"Okay."

"I love *you,* Prima" Nico looked away from me, waiting for me to respond. When I didn't, he left.

I didn't know how I felt about Nico right now.

All I knew was that I couldn't forgive him.

Gianna Marie Ferraro

AUDREY

The trees at the park by Andrés's house were green and lush, getting ready for the summer months, but the sky was overcast.

I sat on the swings with Andrés. We normally met somewhere by his house. It was safer there.

"What happened to Coy?" Andrés questioned. "I saw he had a black eye."

"Dad beat the shit out of him. Tried to steal money, I guess," I explained.

"Jeez, what would your old man do if he found out about me?" He chuckled nervously.

"He won't find out about you," I insisted.

He grabbed my hand gently and gave it a kiss. I placed my hand on his cheek before kissing him softly.

"I love you too much to let him hurt you," I whispered.

"But you can't promise anything," he told me. "You can't control him."

He was probably right. No one could control Dad.

"Don't say that. We just need to keep it a secret for now."

"Audrey, I don't want to keep our relationship a secret." Andrés frowned.

"We have to. I can't let him find out."

"Why? Or he'll hurt me? Something you said you'll make sure he won't do?" Andrés kept hold of my hand and looked at me.

"I don't know. Let's stop talking about this." I shook my head.

"Audrey, I love you and I care about you." He squeezed my hand. "I don't want you to get hurt, but I don't want to hide our relationship anymore."

I didn't want to hide it anymore either.

"Maybe after school we can leave . . . together. When we graduate."

"What about my mom?" Andrés questioned.

"Right . . . maybe we can take her with us?"

Andrés took care of his mother. I had never met the woman, but I knew she was older. Andrés was the youngest of three and had agreed to take care of her after his older siblings moved out.

"Would you be okay with that?" Andrés tilted his head.

"Of course I would." I smiled at him, placing a hand on his cheek. I loved him so much.

prima

Dinner was quiet. Nico slid me a velvet box, much like the one that had held the gold bracelet he gave me before. This time there was a necklace with a silver heart pendant. He gave me a small smile as I took it out of the box.

"Thank you," I told him as I tried to put the necklace on.

Nico got up and helped me put it on. He kissed my cheek softly. "I'm sorry, Prima. For beating Coy. But he needed to learn a lesson."

I was surprised at the apology, even though he didn't seem very apologetic.

"You could've talked to him. You did help raise him. I know you use this kind of punishment in your everyday life, but this is my son, Nico."

"I know, Prima." Nico took his seat. "You have to understand. He tried to steal from me."

"But he failed. He already got punched in the face," I reminded him.

Nico took a moment to respond. "Still."

"Still what?"

"You wouldn't understand."

"How do you know?"

The restaurant had gone quiet. People were murmuring and glancing at our table.

Nico huffed. "Eat your food."

Gianna Marie Ferraro

NICO

I didn't know if Prima could tell my apology was fake. I didn't regret beating the kid up one bit. He had to learn a lesson.

He lived under my roof and still tried to steal from me. I wasn't his father, but I was still his legal guardian. I would do things my way. No one would bat an eye. They couldn't.

Coy was a troubled kid. Part of it was probably my fault. If I hadn't snapped that day at the bowling alley, maybe we could still be a happy family. Those days were over though, and he got what he deserved.

Gianna Marie Ferraro

coy

I could hear water dripping from the ceiling of the abandoned warehouse. The warehouse was on the edge of town near the Hispanic neighborhood. It had been abandoned for years. My small gang found it and took over.

It was filled with a bunch of empty wooden crates. I guessed that's what they used to make here because I couldn't seem to find anything else.

The men with me talked amongst themselves. I stared at the leaky roof. I didn't remember it raining the past few days.

"Coy, what's the plan?" Ricky snapped me out of my trance.

"Well"—I sat down on a wooden box—"we have to get rid of the threat."

"Let's shoot the old man already!" Devon chimed in.

"We can't do that, dumbass." Georgio ran a hand down his face "If we kill him, and they know who did it, we are all dead."

I had a nice group of guys in my gang. They weren't all the smartest, but at least I had a gang. I had my best friend, Ricky, Georgio—who got us most of our supplies—Devon, the airhead, and Gaberiell.

"Georgio is right. We can't just go in and kill Nico." I tapped my foot. "We need a better plan than that."

"We could make it look like an accident," Devon hummed.

"Finally, something smart from you," Ricky scoffed. "Why don't you mess with your old man's car or something?"

"G, can you get us the stuff we need?" I questioned.

"I'll see what I can do. It's going to cost you though," Georgio replied.

"How much?"

"I don't know, five hundred, maybe?"

I let out a puff of air. "Okay, I'll see what I can do."

Five hundred dollars was a shit ton of money. I didn't even think I had a hundred. My mom gave us an allowance every week, but that was only ten dollars, unless we needed something. I needed that money, and I'd get it, even if I had to take it. I had to get rid of Nico.

AUDREY

It was around seven when I got home, which was later than usual. I had lost track of time at the park. I quietly opened the front door. I knew Mom wouldn't be mad if I was home late, but Dad would be.

Mom turned to me and smiled. Thankfully, she was the only one on the couch.

"You're home late," she told me. "Your dinner is in the fridge."

"I lost track of time," I told her.

"Studying with Mary?"

"Yup" I told her before making my way to the kitchen.

I wanted to tell her about Andrés. I really did, but I knew she would say the same thing to me that Coy had. That it was a dumb idea.

After I finished heating up my food, I made my way to the couch and sat next to her. I picked at my peas.

A random question popped into my head. I wanted to get my mind off everything. "Mom, why did you marry dad?" I never knew. I knew there was an age gap, but that was it.

"Why the sudden interest?" Her voice sounded uneasy.

"Just curious." I shoved some peas into my mouth.

"My parents arranged it," she told me.

"They arranged it? Like you didn't have a choice?" I didn't think that many people arranged marriages anymore.

"I had somewhat of a say." She shrugged. "But that doesn't matter. We're here now, and that's that."

I wanted to push, but it didn't seem like she wanted to talk.

Gianna Marie Ferraro

coy

I was lying on my bed in the dark when I heard a knock on the door. "Come in," I huffed as I sat up.

"Why are the lights off?" Audrey questioned as she entered my room.

She was wearing a pink pajama set and matching fuzzy slippers.

"I have a migraine," I told her. "It's also almost eleven."

My head had been hurting since the bar.

I turned my lamp on. "What are you doing awake?"

"I heard you come in. Dad is out and Mom's asleep." Audrey told me.

"Well, goodnight. . . " I went to turn my light off again.

"Did you know Mom and Dad had an arranged marriage?"

I shook my head. "Honestly, no."

The two never mentioned anything about how they met. I guessed it made sense with the age gap.

Audrey sat next to me on the bed. "I'm scared, Coy. Dad has a date set up for me on Friday. What if he wants me to marry the guy?"

It was the first time I was hearing about this, but I guessed that made sense since I hadn't been home much.

"Why are you telling me all of this?" I asked.

Audrey never came to me with any of her problems. Hell, we barely even talked to each other.

"Because you're the only person I feel would understand." Tears pricked her eyes. "Mom won't do shit. You know that."

"You'll be fine. Go to bed."

"You're such an asshole!" Audrey yelled as she hit me with a pillow.

My bedroom door opened slightly. Mom popped her head in. "What's going on?"

"Sorry, did we wake you?" Audrey questioned.

She shook her head. "No, I was just lying down.

"Everything's fine, Mom, go back to sleep." I replied, turning the light before laying back down.

I could hear Audrey mumble to herself as she left the room. I might have been an asshole, but what was I going to do?

CHAPTER TWENTY-NINE

AUDREY

I took small steps as I walked with Andrés. We wanted to have as much time together as possible before I had to be home. I hadn't told Andrés about the date my father set up. I'd been too nervous.

"I need to tell you something." I bit my lip.

"What is it?" Andrés's face switched from calm to worrisome.

I hesitated but replied, "My father set me up with this guy and wants me to go on a date with him tonight. It's one of his friends' kids."

He frowned. "And you can't say no."

"Yeah . . . "

"I understand . . . "

I grabbed his hands gently. "Trust me, I don't want to do it."

"I know you can't disobey your father." He pulled me into a hug.

I pulled away quickly. "We are too close to my house."

"Sorry," he mumbled.

"I'm sorry, Andrés"

His tone shifted slightly. "What does this mean for us? What if you fall for this guy?"

"It's one date. I'm not going to fall for him in one day." I chuckled. "Mom said it was just a date."

I was still worried that it was more than a date after what mom had told me about her marriage being arranged. Why wouldn't they do the same for me?

"It better be." He gave me a small smile.

"Are you getting jealous?" I teased.

"Wouldn't you if I had a date with a random girl?" he questioned.

"I guess."

"Imagine if your mom went on a date with some random man. Your dad would probably be mad," he told me.

"Well, Dad goes on dates without Mom all the time." I puffed. "She knows and I'm pretty sure he knows that she does. Doesn't stop him. I think it bothers her, but I don't know. She doesn't do anything about it."

"Well, your dad is also . . . " he paused. "Interesting."

"Yeah, he sure is interesting." I chuckled.

We arrived at the block before my house. I gave him a gentle smile before giving him a kiss on the cheek. "I'll see you Monday?"

"Wait, I want to give you something." Andrés smiled as he took off his gold chain. A lot of men wore them these days. Hell, even my brother did. He placed it gently around my neck.

"So during your date, you can think of me." His gaze dimmed.

I smiled and gave him another kiss on the cheek, then said, "Thank you" before I walked off.

prima

I woke up from my nap in a cold sweat. I had another nightmare about Ray. Sill was in all my dreams, watching. He was screaming, but I couldn't hear a thing.

I hadn't had nightmares about Ray in years. What was bringing them up now?

The door opening thankfully woke me up. "Mom, I'm home," Audrey called out.

I sat up on the couch. "Welcome home, honey." I yawned. "Don't forget about your date soon."

"I know." She sighed heavily. "I'll go get ready."

I'm glad she didn't notice the flustered expression on my face.

"Have you seen Coy?" I asked her.

"No, not since this morning," she replied as she took off her shoes.

I nodded as I watched her leave the room. Sometimes I wished I could have eyes on him all the time, like Nico did for me.

The phone on the wall started to ring. I hurried to pick it up. "Hey, Prima," my father called from the other end. "Could you come down to the bar? Nico got into a fight. He's drunk and is refusing medical attention."

"What do you mean by medical attention?" I suddenly felt nauseous.

"Well, he needs stitches, and he says he only wants you to do it."

I breathed in. "I'll be there soon."

The bar was oddly quiet when I entered. The bartender pointed to the back room. I opened the door. The lights were turned off. "Hello?" I called out, of course confused. A few moments later, the lights turned on. "Happy Birthday!" a crowd of people shouted.

There were a few friends: Pat and Barb, Rosina and Winnie, along with a few of Nico's friends, and, of course, my father.

I hadn't celebrated my birthday in years. Nico normally would give me something or take me to dinner and call it a day. There was no doubt in my mind that he was trying to make up for what he'd done to Coy.

There were a few balloons and a cake on the table. The cake had "Happy 38th, Prima" written on it. It had been seventeen years since I married Nico. How did time fly by so fast?

Nico came over and gave me a kiss on the cheek. "Happy birthday, baby."

"Thanks." My smile felt fake.

I felt sick. I didn't want to be there. It wasn't even my birthday.

"Why do you look so upset, baby?"

"My birthday isn't for another week, Nico." I stayed calm as I told him.

His face dropped. "No, I swear it's today."

"I know when my own birthday is," I mumbled.

"Well, we can celebrate it early. We have stuff going on next week, anyway." He wrapped an arm around my waist.

NICO

Was I a little embarrassed I'd forgotten Prima's birthday? Yeah, but it didn't matter. She got a party. She should have been happy about that.

She was silent for most of it, occasionally saying 'hi' to someone or answering questions. She barely touched her cake. She was so ungrateful.

I felt a tap on my shoulder. Rich stood behind me. "Mr. DeLuca, I need to talk to you."

"What is it?" I snapped. "I'm trying to enjoy this party."

"I saw your daughter . . . kissing someone. A PR guy," Rich told me quietly.

"Find out where he lives." I lowered my voice.

Rich walked away without another word.

Gianna Marie Ferraro

coy

I came home to an empty house. That was fine with me—I didn't want to deal with anyone. It was the third of the month which meant Mom got her allowance of seven hundred dollars. She never spent it all. She always gave some of it to us and probably put the rest away. She always told Nico it was too much money, and he would tell her she needed to spend it.

I had to grab it before she put it in her hiding spot. I peeked into her room, hoping the envelope was still on Nico's desk. I let out a sigh of relief when I saw that it was.

I opened the envelope and took out the five hundred I needed to give Georgio. I knew she was going to notice, but I didn't care. Maybe she would think that Nico shorted her this month.

I shoved the money into my jacket pocket and slipped back into my room before I heard shouting. I shut my door and opened the window, ready to slip out.

"Why are you so mad, Prima?" Nico groaned. "I tried, okay?!"

"You can't even get my own birthday right! Nico, you were a week off. Not a few days. A week!"

Mom shouted. "God, Nico, you don't even care about me."

Everything went quiet for a moment, and I slipped out my window.

Gianna Marie Ferraro

prima

My face stung. Nico had slapped me.

Nico's face showed remorse when I finally looked at him ."Prima, baby"—he went to touch my arm, but I backed away— "I didn't mean to."

I made my way to the bedroom without another word. I grabbed a bag and started to throw clothes in it.

"Prima, what are you doing?"

"Leaving."

"And where would you be going?" He grabbed me from behind. His hands felt so big. I felt so small.

I froze for a moment. Where would I go? A hotel? I didn't have any money of my own. My dad's? He would probably send me right back here.

"I don't know, Nico. I don't know, okay?" my voice shook.

"I didn't mean to hit you, baby." He wrapped his arms around my waist gently. "I'm sorry."

The tone of his voice felt shallow. He couldn't make eye contact with me.

"Why don't you have Enzo take you shopping or something?" Nico pulled out his wallet. "This will be extra for this month."

"I don't want your money, Nico, leave me alone, please." I ripped out of his grasp.

"What do I have to do to please you!" I could tell that Nico was losing his patience.

"This is why I fucked Sill. He actually cared for me!"

"I swear, bitch, I'll fucking hit you again."

"At least he *cared* about me." Tears released, spilling down my cheeks.

"It's been years. Let it go! He's dead!" Nico grabbed my shoulder.

"Mom?" Audrey was standing at the door.

"Prima, why don't you help Audrey get ready for her date tonight." Nico huffed before storming off, pushing his way past Audrey.

I wiped a tear and put on a fake smile. "Yeah, let's get you ready."

Audrey shuffled a bit before making her way to her room. I followed shortly after.

She sat down at her makeup table, pulling out a few things. "Mom"—she hesitated—"who's Sill?"

"An old friend." I grabbed her hairbrush and started to brush her hair. She stayed quiet. I was glad she didn't push for more information.

"Do I have to go tonight?" She pouted.

"I know you don't want to, sweetie" I plastered on a fake grin . I noticed a new necklace around her neck but ignored it. "One date is all your father is asking."

"I know," she huffed. "What if it's more than one date?"

We went silent as we could hear Nico yelling in the other room. I didn't think either of us could make out what he was saying. The phone slammed, followed by the door.

"What was that all about?" Audrey looked at me.

"I don't know. He's in a bad mood."

"Did he hit you?" she asked quietly.

"Let's make sure you look good tonight." I ignored her question.

"Mom, I'm not a kid. Did he hit you?"

"He was frustrated. I pushed his buttons."

"Doesn't mean he should hit you." She crossed her arms. "Did you really cheat on him?" she whispered.

I stayed quiet for a moment. "It was a long time ago."

I could feel tears once again swell up in my eyes. I hadn't thought about Sill in years. I tried to keep him pushed in the back of my mind. All I could think about was Sill getting dragged out by Nico. I didn't know if I could forgive him for that.

AUDREY

Mom ignored the rest of my questions as I got ready. We picked out a navy-blue dress with a white belt for my date. She told me the guy I was seeing was named Monte Giordano.

The restaurant was one my parents frequented. I had only been there a handful of times. It felt outdated and smelled like cigarette smoke.

I glanced around the restaurant, ready to get this over with. A guy around my age was sitting at a table alone. He was wearing a brown suede jacket, blue jeans, and an orange knit shirt. He wore glasses with silver rims that framed his face. His brown hair was slicked back, contrasting the rest of his modern outfit.

He waved me over with a grin. I knew he had seen me, but I'd never seen him. "Audrey?"

"Yeah, that's me." I dawdled over to the table and sat down.

"I'm Monte." He grinned. "Wow, you are just as pretty as your picture. And even prettier than watching you from a distance."

"Why did you want to go on a date with me?" I questioned bluntly.

Monte chuckled. "Can we at least get to dinner first before we get to the hard hitters?" He smiled. "My pops and your father wanted us to get to know each other."

"So, it was their idea . . . "

"Yeah, well, I saw you one day with your dad." He flipped through the menu. "I thought it couldn't hurt to meet you."

"So, this isn't an arranged marriage then." I let out a sigh of relief.

He snickered. "They really told you nothing."

"I was told I had to go on a date and that was it. I didn't even know your name until ten minutes ago."

"Funny." Monte set down the menu. "How old are you again?"

"Sixteen in October." I glanced at the menu. "You?"

"Eighteen."

I'm not going to lie. Monte wasn't a bad looking guy. His jaw was chiseled, and he seemed fit. He also had a nice smile.

He called the waiter over and we both ordered. I didn't like that he ordered for me, but I stayed quiet. Both of us stayed silent for a while.

"You really didn't want to come here, did you? Are you seeing someone or something?"

I stayed quiet, debating on how to answer. "That's really none of your business."

"It kinda is," Monte told me. "Your father wants us to get married before next year."

"You said this wasn't a marriage thing." I stood up.

"I said no such thing, hun. I said that our parents wanted us to go on a date." He sipped his water. "Not that we weren't engaged. Now sit down. The food is going to be here."

I sat back down, but I felt like I was suffocating. I needed to get out of there and fast. What would that do?

He wanted us to get married before the end of next year? I guessed I would be eighteen by then since I was turning seventeen in October. My worst fear was coming true, and no one would listen to me. This was happening too soon.

NICO

I tried to forget my argument with Prima. I had bigger problems to deal with. Rich had given me the address of Audrey's little boyfriend's house faster than I expected.

"Enzo, come with me," I demanded.

"Yes, sir." He seemed hesitant, but I knew he wouldn't defy me.

We made our way out of the bar and into Enzo's car. The ride was quiet until Enzo broke the silence.

"Hey, Nico . . . "

"What's wrong?" I groaned.

"What are you going to do to the kid? scare him?"

I hadn't thought that far ahead. He was dating my daughter, at least I assumed. But she was going to marry Monte whether she liked it or not. There was no way in hell I would let her marry anyone who wasn't her kind. She was my only kid. I couldn't fuck that up.

"Yeah, scare him," I told him.

Gianna Marie Ferraro

coy

I was on my way back from giving Georgio the money when I saw Nico and Enzo coming out of his car. Nico normally didn't go to this side of town, so why was he here?

Then I saw him. The dude my sister had been seeing was sitting on his front porch. He noticed them coming and quickly stood up.

"Don't move, kid." Nico's voice was like daggers. "Are you the little beaner kissing my daughter? Right on our street?"

"Mr. DeLuca, I can explain—"

Before he could even finish, Enzo had grabbed him by the collar, slamming him in the jaw with his fist.

"Explain? Some of my guys saw you two kissing. She's engaged, did you know that?"

"What, I—"

Nico didn't hesitate to pull out his gun. He blew the kid's brains out all over the porch.

"Nico, you said we were going to scare him! What the fuck!" Enzo groaned.

My heart sank thinking of Audrey. I had warned her, but I could've stopped him. I should've stopped him. *Why didn't I do anything?*

I wasn't thinking as I ran toward the men, ramming into Nico's side as hard as I could, pushing him to the ground. Nico looked up at me, stunned.

"The fuck are you doing here?!" he roared. "You want to die too, boy?" Nico got off the ground, wiping off his pants before landing his fist in my jaw.

I groaned in pain, grabbing my jaw. "Why would you kill him?"

"That's none of your damn business," Nico hissed.

"Nico, come on, leave the kid alone," Enzo urged. "Someone probably heard the gunshots. We need to get out of here."

Nico punched me one more time, this time sending me to the ground. I felt something land on my chest as he ran at the sound of sirens.

I must have blacked out for a moment. When I sat up, his car was already gone. A police car was in its place. Something had fallen on my lap as I sat up. I picked it up slowly. It was Nico's gun.

"Put the gun down!" the officer shouted as he got out of his car, firearm in hand.

I dropped it quickly. "It's not mine! I didn't do it!"

"Get up! Hands behind your head!" he shouted.

"Officer, it's a misunderstanding." My voice shook.

"Yeah, a dead kid behind you is a real misunderstanding." The officer kept his gun pointed at me.

I looked around for a moment. The officer was all alone. I had two choices: I could go with the officer and let Nico frame me for murder, or I could do something about it.

I grabbed the gun and quickly aimed it at the officer's leg, shooting him. His gun went off as well. I didn't even feel the bullet hit my shoulder as I ran.

I ran until I came across somewhere familiar. I felt dizzy and out of breath. I placed a hand on my bleeding shoulder, and warm blood coated my hand.

"Coy, what happened to you?" a familiar voice queried.

Grandpa grabbed my side, helping me into his home. How did I get all the way to this side of town? Was I really running that long?

He set me down on my couch before grabbing a bag from a cabinet. "What the hell did you get yourself into, my boy?"

I stayed quiet and let him dress the wound. All my life, the men around me had taught me that family was everything. But I couldn't even trust my own grandfather. He was one of Nico's right-hand men, after all, but he was still family.

Once he finished, he asked, "Nico shot you?"

"No . . . the police did." I sniffled. "I shot him first."

"Well, shit, kid." Grandpa chuckled.

"You aren't going to tell Nico I'm here?" I stared at my feet, trying to ignore the stinging pain in my shoulder.

He shook his head. "No, I'm not."

Grandpa got off the couch, grabbing a bottle of whisky off his counter. He poured out two glasses. He handed me one and said, "You are going to need this for the pain."

I took a sip, letting it burn my throat. I had had whisky before, not with family, of course.

"You should get out of here," he started. "You can stay the night, but tomorrow, I think you should head to your aunt's. Nico and the police are probably looking for you."

I had never met my aunt. I didn't think mom ever told me her name. She didn't like to talk about her sisters, and I didn't know why.

"Can I say goodbye to Audrey and Mom?" My voice quivered.

"You shot a cop, kid. I don't think you should." Grandpa ran a hand down his face. "I'll tell them where you went. You have to get on the first bus out of here in the morning, got it?"

He was right. I was in deep shit. There wasn't much I could do. It hurt not being able to say goodbye to my family.

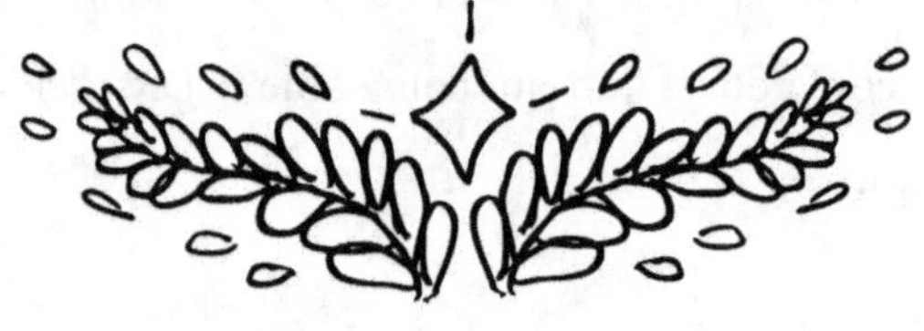

AUDREY

Monte offered to drive me home. I wanted to walk, but he insisted it was too dark.

"Do you even want to marry me?" I finally asked him.

"Why not? You're pretty enough."

What the hell was that supposed to mean? I needed to get out of this car.

He waited a moment before saying, "Yeah, I think you'll make a great wife."

I wanted to jump out of the car. I wanted to say something, but nothing came out.

"You'll serve your purpose," he mumbled, but I heard him.

"I think you'll make a great wife," he repeated with a smile.

NICO

"Nico, this is fucking insane." Enzo gripped. "Are you really framing him?"

"Better him than me," I replied as I drove. I pressed my foot harder on the gas.

"Nico, I know you have your issues with the kid." He let out a breath. "But he will go to jail. Then he could rat you out."

Would he rat me out? No. He knew he would be dead if he did. I had guys in there.

I stayed quiet and drove.

Enzo stared out the window in silence. I don't think he knew what to say.

"Get out," I told him once we parked in front of his apartment.

"Goodnight, Nico." Enzo glanced back at me before exiting the car.

Why could no one see I could have Ray's replacement child out of my life for good? I needed Coy gone, and this was the only way to do it without whacking him. Prima would never forgive me for this.

Gianna Marie Ferraro

prima

Audrey told me about her date when she got home. My heart ached to think Nico wanted her to marry this man, and he didn't even tell me.

Audrey buried her face in the couch pillow, her knees to her chest as she screamed in it for a moment. "I can't believe him!"

I frowned and let out a heavy sigh. I brought my attention to the front door when Nico entered. His shirt was splattered in blood and he had a sour look on his face.

"What happened to you?" I questioned, getting off the couch.

"Coy got arrested," Nico spat. "For murder."

Shock ran through my body. "What?!" I hurried over to him. "Murder? What do you mean?!"

"I saw the whole thing. He was pissed. He saw the guy kiss Audrey." Nico grabbed my arms. "I tried to stop him. That's why there's blood on my shirt."

"Andrés?" Audrey gasped.

"You shouldn't have been kissing him back," Nico spat. "Maybe your brother had the right to do it."

Audrey didn't say anything. She ran to her room. I could hear her sobs through the walls.

Something was off. Coy wouldn't kill anyone. He was troubled, but he wouldn't kill anyone. Especially not someone Audrey was seeing. He cared about her too much.

I turned my attention to Nico, frustrated tears in my eyes. "What did you do? First, you arrange a marriage for Audrey without me, and now my son is arrested."

"Don't ask questions you don't want the answers to." Nico poured himself a drink.

"You killed the kid, didn't you?" I crossed my arms over my chest.

I knew Nico better than that. Lying was how he talked.

He stayed silent and took a sip of his drink.

"Why do you hate Coy so much?! Why did you have to frame him for something you did?"

"You don't know anything, Prima." His voice was low.

"I know you, Nico. I may be quiet, but I listen. I watch. I know you, Nico!" I shouted.

"Lots of talk for someone so quiet." Nico finished his drink, setting down the glass.

AUDREY

Was Andrés really dead, or was dad trying to provoke me? Did Coy really kill him? Why would he do that? I couldn't stop sobbing. I felt like I was suffocating in my little room. I hurried to open a window.

I could hear Mom and Dad arguing. Mom must've had the window open in the living room.

"You killed the kid, didn't you?" Mom sounded pissed.

It was quiet before mom began shouting again. *Did Dad kill him?* I could feel my face turn red.

My bedroom door opened for a second. Dad's bloody shirt was thrown inside. My heart was beating as I walked over to it. It was too real. That was his blood, wasn't it?

I sniffled. I could hear other voices coming from the other room. I pushed my ear against the door.

Gianna Marie Ferraro

prima

There was a knock on the door. It was late. Who would come here this late?

Nico took his blood-stained shirt off, throwing it at me before going to answer the door in his undershirt. I threw the shirt into Audrey's room, not having much time to hide it.

"May I help you, officer?" Nico crossed his arms over his chest.

"Yeah, we are looking for Coy DeLuca," the officer told him, "May we come in?"

I didn't see the second police officer until Nico let them inside. One tilted his hat to me. "Ma'am." He smiled. "Sorry for coming so late."

I had seen these two officers here before—Officers Young and Ernest. They were the ones who'd tried to get Nico to confess to killing Ray's son. They both had aged, their hair now gray.

"So, you're looking for Coy this time?" Nico sat on the couch. "Prima, go get these gentlemen some coffee."

I knew Nico was trying to get me out of the room so I wouldn't say anything. I put on a fake smile and made my way to the kitchen, trying to eavesdrop the best I could.

"What did Coy do now?" Nico asked them. "It has to be bad if you came here this late at night."

Young started, "He shot a cop. Hit him right in the artery. He's in critical condition. We don't know if he is going to make it through the night."

"Thankfully, the officer was able to call for help. He recognized Coy as your son. But Coy was also found at a crime scene," Ernest added.

"I see." Nico scratched his chin. "I haven't seen him since this morning. I'm not surprised he killed someone."

I set the coffee on the coffee table and stood near the entrance to the kitchen.

"Liar!" I heard Audrey shouting. "*Liar*!"

I hurried into the living room. Audrey was standing in front of the men, Nico's bloody shirt in hand. She threw it at one of the cops.

"I heard you talking to Mom. You killed Andrés." I heard Audrey screech. "You killed him didn't you!"

"Nico, we never said he killed anyone," Officer Young interjected.

Officer Ernest examined the shirt. "Well, maybe we are looking for two DeLucas."

"Let's go downtown, Nico, shall we?" Ernest demanded.

Nico pulled a gun from between the couch cushions. *How long had that been there?* He rushed over to me, putting the gun to my head. I didn't feel an ounce of fear. I knew he wouldn't shoot me.

"You want me to shoot her? Huh? Come on, Audrey, why did you have to pull that shit?" Nico growled.

"Nico, come on, put the gun down," Officer Young replied calmly.

Nico didn't hesitate. He shot the officer right in the chest, the other in the head. My ears rang as Audrey screamed. My throat felt like it was closing.

"Audrey! Get in the car. NOW!" Nico pulled me out the door, pushing me into the front seat of the car. Audrey got in the back seat. I looked back at her. She was shaking.

"You two have been a real pain in my ass." Nico sped out of the driveway. "Can't keep your mouths shut. Do you want me to get arrested?! Do you want to lose everything?"

"Nico, slow down, you're going to hit someone." My heart pounded as I gripped my seat.

"You, Audrey! I should fucking shoot you. Why would you pull that shit?" Nico drove even faster.

"Dad, slow down!" Audrey begged.

"Nico, please, at least let Audrey out of the car." I cried.

AUDREY

The car came to a screeching halt as Dad yelled at me to get out.

"Go, honey, please." Mom sounded calm despite the situation.

I hesitated before getting out of the car. Where was he going to take her? The car screeched away, leaving me alone in the dark.

I walked for a while, thinking of what to do next, before stumbling upon the bar my dad always went to. I could see through the window. Enzo was in there talking to someone.

Once I entered, almost everyone looked at me. Enzo approached me. "Audrey, what are you doing here?"

I couldn't help but start crying again. Enzo wrapped an arm around my shoulders and led me to the back room. He sat me down and handed me water.

"What happened?" Enzo asked again.

"Were you there?" I asked him between sobs. "Is he dead?

Enzo frowned and handed me his handkerchief. He let out a breath. "There are a lot of things I don't want to do but I have too. Now, why are you here?"

"Dad got caught" I blew my nose in the handkerchief. "He took Mom in his car. He was driving so fast. I don't know where they are going. The police came looking for Coy, but I freaked out at Dad. He tried to frame him."

"Why don't I take you to my place, okay?" Enzo gave me a reassuring smile. "I'll find them."

He took me out to his car, and we drove for a while in silence. I looked out the window. The streets were lit by lamplight. People walked on the sidewalks so casually. My world felt like it was falling apart.

We passed by his apartment building. My stomach dropped. Where was he taking me?

He parked the car in front of a bridge. "Your father called me before you arrived. He said, 'if I saw you, to take care of it.'" He couldn't look me in the eyes as he pulled out his gun.

"Uncle Enzo?" I gulped.

"Get out of the car, Audrey," Enzo demanded.

We both got out of the car. He kept the gun pointed at me. I couldn't stop crying. My dad wanted me dead. *Was it because I had ratted him out?*

"Uncle Enzo, please," I begged.

"Turn around, Audrey," Enzo demanded.

"Please, you don't have to do this." I turned around, shaking.

I heard a gunshot but felt nothing. I turned around. Enzo dropped the gun and started to cry. "I can't do it."

I couldn't remember ever seeing Enzo cry. It made me a little uncomfortable.

"I'll find your mom." Enzo wiped his tears. "Go back to my place. It's only a few blocks away."

I watched Enzo leave before making my way back. I was still shaking. He'd been ordered to kill me. Was dad going insane?

I couldn't help but let tears stream down. Andrés was dead and I had no clue where Coy or mom were. I felt so lost.

The walk to the apartment building must have taken at least five minutes, but it felt like seconds. I was consumed with my thoughts.

I knocked on the door of their apartment. Pat answered a few moments later, her hair in rollers and her robe on. "Audrey, what are you doing here?"

We sat on the couch and I broke down, telling her everything that had happened. I tried to be quiet so I wouldn't wake Frankie.

"Is all of this my fault?" I asked her. "I told the cops about Dad."

"No, honey. Was it smart? No." Pat pulled me into a warm hug. "If anything, it sounds like your dad is going batshit crazy."

"He wanted to kill me. What if he kills Mom?"

"Let's not worry about that now, okay? Your mom is tough. She's been through worse." She got off the couch. "I'll grab you a blanket and pillow. You can sleep on the couch for the night."

NICO

I took Prima to a motel where the family was supposed to meet if I got in trouble. She watched me as I paced the room with a cheap bottle of bourbon.

"You've never ratted on me, Prima." I took a swig from the bottle. "But my own daughter did." I cackled. "Why would she do that?"

"You killed her boyfriend and tried to frame her brother and my son." Prima's voice was calm.

It fucking pissed me off how calm she was. Why wasn't she freaking out? I had to take care of this situation. My family betrayed me.

I picked up the phone and dialed a number. "Enzo, yeah, I need you to do something for me. Take care of Audrey, will you? Why? She ratted, that's why. Do your damn job!"

Prima's eyes widened. "She's your daughter, Nico."

"Not anymore." I finished the bottle, then wiped my mouth on my arm.

She got off the bed, slipping her shoes on.

"What are you doing?" I sent her a glare.

"Leaving." Her voice shook. She was scared. Good.

"Like hell you are." I stepped in front of the door.

"I've dealt with your shit for seventeen years, Nico, but I will not let you kill my daughter."

I could feel the anger coming out. I grabbed her arms tightly, throwing her onto the bed, causing her to hit her head on the headboard. "You aren't going to do shit! You are going to stay the perfect wife I was promised."

Gianna Marie Ferraro

prima

I felt dizzy as I tried to sit up, but he pushed me back down. I struggled, kicking and screaming, as he pinned me down with one arm. He used the other to take off his tie, using it to tie my hands to the headboard.

I was panicking. Thoughts of Ray flooded my mind. I tried to shake it, I had to save Audrey.

"Nico, please, stop." I was shaking as tears poured out.

He shoved a rag into my mouth, staring me into my soul. "You will not leave me. I *need* you, Prima." His voice cracked before he lay next to me, holding me on the bed.

CHAPTER THIRTY

PRIMA

The sound of knocking startled me awake. My head was throbbing. Nico groaned as he got off the bed. He untied my hands before tying them behind my back, securing the tie tightly around my wrists. He picked me up, then set me down in the closet. We heard the knock again. "Stay quiet," he told me before going to the door.

I tried to peek through a small crack in the door, keeping silent. I could only see a sliver of light which didn't do much.

I heard the door open. "Enzo, what are you doing here?"

"You said we would meet here if anything got dicey," Enzo reminded him.

"Right. Did you take care of it?"

"Yeah, I did." He cleared his throat. "Where's Prima?"

"The closet."

"Why is she in the closet?"

"Don't worry about that. Why are you here?"

"thought I'd check in on you, that's all." Enzo sounded nervous.

"Are you wearing a wire?"

"No, Nico, I'm not wearing wire." Enzo groaned.

NICO

"The fact that you wanted me to kill your kid is fucked up, Nico." His voice shook slightly.

Enzo was sweating. *Was he nervous?*
I rolled my eyes. "Stop complaining."

It wasn't like I had wanted to kill Audrey. I *had* to. It was the only way to keep her mouth shut.

"That kid of yours is making you soft," I told him. "You've worked for me for years. You know how I do things. Keep your mouth shut or suffer the consequences."

"So, what's the plan now?" Enzo replied in a calmer tone.

"Probably start heading farther from the city."
I didn't ignore the fact Enzo was sweating. I almost pulled a gun out on him. I felt a sharp pain and fell to the ground before I could do anything.

Gianna Marie Ferraro

prima

I messed with the tie around my wrists. It wasn't very hard to slip out of it since it was silk. I took the towel out of my mouth and took a deep breath.

I glanced around the closet. Nico had been throwing his empty bottles into it. I picked one up and, without thinking, pushed myself out of the closet. I slammed the bottle right on Nico's forehead as hard as I could. Nico ended up falling backward, hitting the wall and making a dent.

My heart was racing. What had I done? He wasn't dead, was he? The groan he made proved he wasn't.

Enzo looked just as shocked as I felt. Nico felt his forehead. Blood was dripping down it. "You Bitch!"

The door busted open, and two police officers crashed in. Did Enzo rat him out? *Why?* Were they looking for Enzo?

They checked me out at the hospital before taking me down to the station for questioning. They said I had a mild concussion.

My head was pounding as I waited in a room with Enzo. He was tapping his foot.

"Why?" was all I could say.

Enzo ran a hand through his hair. "The moment Nico told me he wanted me to kill his own daughter, I lost all respect for that man. That was the first time I ever disobeyed orders."

"So, you didn't . . . " I stopped breathing for a moment.

"Of course I didn't." He reassured me. "She's here for questioning. They picked her up after I said I'd lead them to Nico."

"Have you seen Coy?" I asked with urgency.

"No, I haven't. The kid could be anywhere."

I placed my head in my hands.

The room was so quiet you could hear a pin drop. We both turned our heads to the sound of footsteps. Audey was walking down the hall. I barely remembered moving, but before I knew it, she was in my arms. I let tears stream down my cheeks.

"Are you okay, baby?" I sniffled.

"Yeah, I'm okay."

"Mrs. DeLuca, we need you for questioning now," a man's voice rang down the hall.

NICO

If Prima hadn't hit me with that bottle, those cops would never have gotten those handcuffs on me. I was about to face a long court battle. Thankfully, I had a good lawyer.

My family had ratted on me. I had to make a choice. I could kill them. But not Prima. I had to keep Prima alive. I cared about her too much. She was my family. She was my only family.

They put me in jail with no bail. I guessed shooting a cop was a big deal. Killing one was even worse.

I had friends on the inside. So jail would be a breeze as long as I kept my connections. I would get out one day. They'd see what would happen then.

CHAPTER THIRTY-ONE

Prima

Nico sat in front of me, at the other side of the table. He was in an orange jumpsuit and his hands were cuffed.

"Hi, Nico." I didn't know what else to say.

"Prima." He grabbed my hands.

"No touching," the officer behind him hissed.

Nico pulled away and glared at the officer. Then he turned back to face me. "How's Audrey?"

"Why do you care?" I snapped. "Coys gone, not that you would care about that either."

"I care about you, Prima, that's why I ask."

"Do you?"

He leaned in. "The only reason I'm not having someone kill you is because I care about you."

Nico could do anything, even from jail. I had spent a few sleepless nights wondering when Nico would send someone after me. No wonder I was still alive.

"I'll take care of you." Nico leaned back. "You know that. That was my deal to your sweet mother. I'm not going to break it. It's Enzo who has to watch his back, but I heard he skipped town already." He paused. "Where are you staying?"

We were in a hotel outside of town. I wasn't going to tell him that. "Don't worry about it."

The officer behind us stood, oddly quiet. He was allowing Nico to talk so freely but wouldn't let him touch me. Did Nico have a grasp on the guards too?

"Without me—" Nico leaned in "—you'd be dead."

Gianna Marie Ferraro

EPILOGUE

coy

I got off the bus with my stomach in knots. I looked at the address in my hand. I didn't even know if Aunt Stella knew I was coming.

I started walking. Gafton was where I had to go, and I had no clue how to get there.

I took in the air. It was clean. You could see the sky. It was beautiful.

More of the Replacement series

Book 1

Book 2

out July 18th 2026

book 3
out in 2027